Jacob and Isaac

"I'll stay home with Jacob today, Ma," Isaac offered.

"No, you won't," Jacob said. He glared up at Isaac's eager face. "It's a very bad idea."

"I don't understand you," his mother said. "Why is it such a bad idea if your brother stays home and takes care of you?"

"Because . . . because . . . because he'll be good to me! He'll talk to me! He'll read to me. He'll tell me jokes. He'll turn on the television. He'll switch the channels for me. He'll heat up the soup and hold the spoon for me!" He pointed a finger at Isaac, as if accusing him of some horrible crime. "He'll take care of me!"

Isaac responded to the accusation with a proud smile.

"Ma, when he takes care of me, he . . . he makes me feel like a sick person. Ma, if he stays home, I'm going to school. And I'm walking up to every kid I see with a runny nose, watery eyes, and a cough, and I'm going to ask them to breathe on me."

"Jacob, sometimes I really don't think you have a very good idea of what's best for you," his mother said.

DAVID GETZ

.

THIN AIR

HarperTrophy
A Division of HarperCollins*Publishers*

For my lovely wife, Jacqui

*I would also like to thank
my mother, father, and sister;
Paula Danziger and June Foley;
my students at P.S. 166;
and my hamster, Mungo Park,
who stayed up through the night
to keep me company.*

THIN AIR

1

The Night Sky over Kansas cost $1.98. Though it would leave him with only two cents, Jacob felt it was worth it. He could use it for a practical joke on his older brother, Isaac. And it was the whole sky. It was the moon, Mercury, Venus, Mars, Jupiter, and Saturn. It was all the constellations. It was three hundred stars, the Milky Way, and Halley's Comet. It was all some farm boy in Kansas could see if he stood out in the middle of his wheat field on a clear August night and looked up.

Jacob would attach the pieces of the Sky onto the ceiling above Isaac's bunk. Each stick-on planet, star, and galaxy was guaranteed to glow in the dark. Isaac wouldn't notice anything while his light was on. But when he turned it off, his ceiling would fly backwards toward infinity, and the entire universe would open up above him.

Isaac would be frightened, but it might give him and Jacob something to talk about for a change.

Standing on his toes in front of a display of cookbooks for cat owners, Jacob lifted the Night Sky into the air so that the clerk behind the counter could see it. The clerk, whose bald head was shaped like a light bulb, leaned over the counter and brought his face within an inch of Jacob's.

1

The clerk's eyes bulged. He had a long, wispy mustache. He smelled like the basement of Jacob's building. Jacob's nose itched. He scratched it with the corner of the Sky. He put his two dollars down on the counter.

"It's our last Sky," the clerk said.

"I won't drop it," Jacob promised.

Out on the crowded, noisy street, surrounded by all of Manhattan, Jacob clutched the package to his chest. He was surprised by how light the Sky felt in his hands. He was delighted. He had something to look forward to again.

He had gone to sleep the night before looking forward to his first day of sixth grade in his new school and showing his parents he could succeed in a regular class. But he got an asthma attack in the middle of the night. He sprang upright in his bed, trying to wake, gasping for air. He was wheezing and coughing. Not for the first time, he thought he was dying. Slowly he began to wake. He took his asthma spray. He started his breathing exercises. He needed to relax.

Isaac helped by panicking. He scrambled down from his top bunk and sat at the edge of Jacob's bed, looking bug-eyed and pale. He was wearing his blue Rangers jersey, number eleven.

"How come you don't sleep with the helmet on too?" Jacob asked, pulling his knees up to his chest. He breathed out slowly. He coughed. He told himself that if he relaxed, if he stopped wheezing, he could make it to school in the morning.

Isaac called for their mother. He started to dial all of the emergency numbers at once.

"When was the last time you took your theophylline?" Isaac asked. His voice was deep for a fourteen-year-old's.

2

He sounded almost like their father, except their father never panicked.

"Call 555-1313," Jacob gasped.

Isaac quickly dialed the number.

It was Sportsphone.

"How did the Mets do?" Jacob asked, still wheezing.

"Ma!" Isaac called. He hung up the phone. "Jacob, what's Dr. Grophy's number at St. Vincent's Hospital?"

Their mother rushed into the room.

"Ma, he's wheezing," Isaac said, going over to the closet to get his clothes.

Jacob took another inhalation from his spray.

"Jacob, are you all right?" his mother asked.

Holding his breath, keeping the medicine inside him, Jacob nodded yes. He was almost enjoying himself. Watching Isaac in a frenzy distracted him from his own problem: breathing. Isaac's performance, his mother rushing in, first to help him, then to calm Isaac, made him think of his routine asthma attack as an exciting, amusing movie. It even made him laugh, until he began to worry about its star.

"Isaac, where are you going?" his mother asked.

Isaac had put his baseball jacket on over his jersey. Jacob was surprised at how tall his brother was, nearly a head taller than their mother.

"Are we going to the hospital?" Isaac asked.

"Why don't *you* go like that," Jacob suggested. Isaac was still wearing his jockey shorts. "I'll meet you there later." He put his head on the pillow. He was going back to sleep. He did not want to be tired for his first day of school.

When Jacob's alarm sounded at seven, he was already

dressed. Though tired and weak, he was still eager to get to school. He was going to be in a regular class, not that Special 10 class his parents wanted him to be in. They had completed the enrollment papers just before moving from their Lower East Side neighborhood to the Upper West Side.

"I'm not going into any special program," Jacob had told his parents. "There's nothing special about me."

"Jacob, it's a great program," his mother had argued. "It's designed especially for kids like you who miss too much school."

"It's only for bright kids," his father said.

"Bright kids like you, who have chronic illnesses."

"I don't have a chronic illness," Jacob argued. "I'm the same as everybody else. I just have asthma."

"Jacob, you missed over forty days of school last year," his mother said.

"I'll miss more if you put me in that class," Jacob threatened. "I won't go. I'm not ill."

His parents backed down. His father agreed to bring him over to P.S. 89 to register him in a regular class in the sixth grade. But it would be an experiment. If his health held up, if it didn't look as if he was going to miss too many days of school, he could stay.

Getting dressed, to Jacob, meant getting ready to prove himself. In his new school nobody would know he had asthma. Nobody would treat him as if he were disabled. He would be a new kid. He began to lace up his new black high-tops.

"Jacob, where are you going?" his mother asked, entering his room.

"School?" he guessed.

"I don't think that's a very good idea."

"Why not?" he asked. "Lots of kids do it. It keeps them out of trouble."

"I don't think you should exert yourself," she said, sitting down beside him. "It might trigger another attack."

"But . . ."

It was too late. She began The Speech.

"Jacob, you have sensitive lungs," she said, "and you probably have a germ. If you go to school, your germ is going to get a chance to meet all of those other germs hiding out in those other kids in your class. Those kids could be walking germ factories. I'm sure their mothers don't even think twice of sending their kids to school with a germ."

"Ma, what do you think they do?" Jacob asked. "Pack it with their lunches?"

"Pneumonia, strep throat, the flu, doesn't worry these mothers."

"But, Ma . . ."

"Look, Jacob. If you do have a germ—and I don't think we can take a chance, not with you—your germ is definitely going to be the type that invites all those other germs living happily in those other kids to come over to your lungs to have a party."

"But, Ma . . ."

"And suddenly there's going to be a party in your chest, and you're going to get your bronchitis, and instead of a day, you're going to miss the first two weeks of school."

"But . . ."

"You have to stay away from potential infections."

"But those potential infections are my potential friends!"

She ordered him to stay in bed, to rise only to take a

glass of apple juice or some chicken soup from the pot. "This way, you'll only miss one day," she said, pouring the apple juice into six eight-ounce glasses, which she placed in the refrigerator. She removed a frozen chunk of "emergency" soup and placed it in a sauce pan on the stove.

"I'm going to school tomorrow," Jacob insisted.

"I'll stay home with him today, Ma," Isaac offered.

Jacob looked up. He had almost forgotten his brother. Then he realized Isaac had been there all along, quietly waiting for his opportunity to be the wonderful older brother.

"No, you won't," Jacob said.

"It's only the first day of school, Jacob," his mother said. "Maybe it's not such a bad idea."

"It's a bad idea," Jacob said, glaring up at Isaac, whose broad shoulders and eager face reminded Jacob of some sheriff's son in a western. He was wearing their father's old tattered junior-varsity hockey jacket. "It's a very bad idea."

"No, I'll enjoy it," Isaac said, removing his jacket and putting down his books. "We'll have a good time."

"But not too good of a time," his mother cautioned.

"Put your jacket back on, Isaac," Jacob ordered. "Go to school. You have your after-school hockey tryouts today."

"No, it's okay," Isaac said, hanging up his jacket. "They last all week."

"Don't hang up that jacket, Isaac."

"I don't understand you," his mother said, sitting down beside him. She rubbed his back. "Why is it such a bad idea if your brother stays home and takes care of you?"

"Because . . . because . . . because he'll be good to me! He'll talk to me! He'll read to me. He'll tell me jokes. He'll turn on the television. He'll switch the channels for me. He'll heat up the soup and hold the spoon for me!" He pointed a finger at Isaac, as if accusing him of some horrible crime. "He'll take care of me!"

Isaac responded to the accusation with a proud smile. "You want me to take down Blue Line Hockey from the closet?" he asked.

"See!" Jacob cried out in frustration. "He enjoys it! It makes him happy. He enjoys taking care of me!"

"Now, why is that bad?" his mother asked, looking confused.

"Because, Ma, when he takes care of me, he . . . he makes me feel like a sick person."

"But you are," his mother sighed. "You probably have a germ."

"Ma, if he stays home, I'm going to school. And I'm walking up to every kid I see with a runny nose, watery eyes, and a cough, and I'm going to ask them to breathe on me."

"Jacob, sometimes I really don't think you have a very good idea of what's best for you," his mother said.

"I don't need somebody to hold my spoon."

Isaac took his jacket out of the closet and picked up his books. "You sure you don't want me to stay home and play Blue Line?" he asked.

"Go to school, Isaac," Jacob said.

"Look, Jacob, I'm putting your medicines here," his mother said, sitting down on the bed beside him. She removed two pills from their childproof vials and placed them on top of the *Mad* magazines on his desk. "I wrote down when you're supposed to take them."

Jacob turned away and stared at the wall. "I'll take the two pills right after breakfast," he announced. "If I start wheezing, I can take the spray."

"Take the two pills right after breakfast," his mother said. "And if you start wheezing, take the spray."

"And your number and Dr. Grophy's number are on the refrigerator. I'll call if I need anything. Now go to work. You're going to be late." He sat up.

"Don't exert yourself, Jacob. I don't want you bringing on another attack. Stay in bed." She kissed him, then turned the television to face his bed. She pulled out the knob to turn the set on, but turned off the volume.

"Why did you do that?" he asked.

"This way, if you want to watch television, all you have to do is turn the volume switch."

"Ma, please go to work. Isaac, go to school. I can take care of myself."

"I'll phone you between classes," Isaac said, holding the door for their mother.

"I'll phone you this morning. And don't get out of bed if you don't have to," his mother said as they left. She locked the door from the outside.

As soon as he heard their footsteps going down the stairs, Jacob got out of bed. He was going to school.

2

It was the first day of school. He couldn't miss it. He couldn't let the year start without him. He'd be late, but at least he'd get there. He'd have to wait a few minutes, though, before he made his escape. His mother could come rushing back to the apartment in five or ten minutes, just to remind him to drink his juice or to use a teaspoon and not a tablespoon for his cough medicine. He turned the television off and took out his favorite sick-day book, *Legends of Crime*. He propped up his pillows, leaned back, and opened to the chapter on Billy the Kid. He began to read about Billy's mother when he remembered he had to eat breakfast if he was going to take his medicine. If he took his pills on an empty stomach, they would make him queasy and nervous. He noticed there was a plate of fruit on the end table. His mother must have put it there when he wasn't looking. He picked up an apple. It fell apart in his hand. His mother had sliced it into tiny, bite-sized sections. He lost his appetite. He also noticed he was wheezing again.

He returned to his book. He read how Billy had been scrawny but dangerous. His wheezing was getting worse. He put the book down and took his spray. His breathing cleared for a minute or two, but then he started to wheeze again. He took another dose of his spray. It didn't work.

If he relaxed, if he did some breathing exercises, maybe he could open his lungs. Then he could go to school. He didn't want to miss lunch. He didn't want to miss being on somebody's team during recess. He sat up straight, his back to the wall. Hugging his knees to his chest, he tried to blow out all of the air in his lungs. He coughed and gasped. He was getting that dry, scratchy feeling inside. Again he hugged his knees to his chest and tried to blow all the air out of his lungs. He couldn't. It was getting difficult to breathe. He didn't want to have another attack. He didn't want to have to call his mother or brother. He didn't want to feel helpless. He took his pills. He would have to wait to see if they worked.

He thought about his father. He was in Chicago, playing the part of Zachary in *A Chorus Line*. He was expected home in two weeks for a short stay. His father said he didn't enjoy being away from his family, but it was the money he earned acting in regional theaters and touring companies that had allowed them to move out of their drug-infested old neighborhood.

"What can I do?" his father would apologize to Jacob every time he packed his bags. "All I can do is act."

It was his father's traveling that paid for Jacob's medicine, his doctor and hospital bills. Jacob understood that, but didn't accept it. His father was his only friend. They went to the movies and museums together, worried about the Rangers and Mets, laughed at the same jokes, and never mentioned his asthma. Sometimes his father even forgot what foods Jacob was allergic to, or when he was supposed to take his medicines. But that was all right. Jacob remembered.

In two weeks his father would be home. Jacob wondered what he could do to convince him to stay?

His heart was racing. His lungs were clear, but his heart was racing.

It was the pills, he reassured himself. His hands were trembling. It was just the pills, he told himself. Yet he was beginning to feel nervous. He tried to read, but he couldn't hold the book still. He was frightened.

He turned on the television for company. People dressed up like chickens and monkeys were jumping up and down, begging for money. He changed the station. "I just spoke to the doctor," a woman whispered. "There are signs of foul play." He changed the channel. Mister Rogers. Mister Rogers was speaking to the camera. Very slowly. "Well . . . isn't that colorful? What do we see? Pie . . . pie . . . and blueberries for pie."

He turned off the set. He put his high-tops back on. He took his baseball jacket from the closet. Realizing he had to put something into his stomach, he grabbed a handful of pretzels from an open bag in the refrigerator and stuffed them into his jacket pocket. He took his keys and left, slamming the door behind him. He ran down the five flights of steps.

Outside, his back against the building, he lifted his face to the sun. It warmed him, calmed him. He listened to the street sounds for companionship. The bickering of cars and trucks, the wailing of an ambulance siren, the sound of salsa music coming from a window above, all helped make him feel less alone.

He began to walk towards school, munching his pretzels. He stopped. His mother and brother were going to call in an hour or so. If he didn't answer the phone, they would both send ambulances and then come flying home.

He decided to get the *Times* before going back upstairs. Maybe the new play his mother was in had been reviewed. He could check to see if the Mets had won.

The Mets had lost. The play wasn't reviewed. Back at his building, he stuck his hands into his jacket pocket and pulled out a handful of pretzel crumbs. His keys were gone. He was locked out. Within an hour his mother and brother would call home. He had to get back into that apartment.

He ran back to the newsstand where he had purchased the *Times*.

"I'm sorry," Jacob said, trying to get the man's attention.

"What are you sorry about? You don't like the news in that paper I sold you?"

"No. I lost my keys."

"So you want a newspaper that tells you where to find them?"

"No. Do you mind if I look through your newspapers to see if they fell out when I paid you?"

"Go ahead and good luck."

"Thanks." Jacob began to sort through the magazines and newspapers. He looked on the ground beneath and on the sides of the booth. No keys.

"You sure you didn't see me drop them?"

"Even if you did drop them, I wouldn't have seen it. I'm blind."

"Oh, I'm sorry," Jacob said, backing away.

"Don't be sorry. Why aren't you in school?"

12

"I had an asthma attack."

"Oh, I'm sorry," the dealer said.

"You don't have to be sorry. I'm all right."

"Me too," said the dealer.

Jacob started walking back home. He couldn't call his mother. Her phone number was on the refrigerator. He wasn't even sure if she was at work or downtown at some theater, rehearsing. And he couldn't call his brother. It would be just another great excuse for Isaac to come to the rescue.

He thought of running away from home. He couldn't. His asthma medicine was back up in the apartment. He couldn't survive the night without it.

He shuddered as he pictured the ambulances, police cars, his mother and brother, all flying towards his building. Imagining the anxious and confused look on his mother's face when she saw him, perfectly happy, sitting on the front steps of his building, made him feel flushed and ashamed.

He would have to call Isaac. The phone booth was in front of the bookstore. He figured he had at least fifteen minutes. They sold used books inside. Maybe he could find something funny, something to make him laugh.

Instead, he found the Night Sky over Kansas.

He also found his keys. They were on the ground, by the phone booth. They must have fallen out of his pocket when he pulled out his change for the newspaper. He ran home.

The phone was ringing as he entered the apartment. He picked it up.

"How's your germ?" It was his mother.

"He's not here right now. Who's calling, please?" he

said as he darted to the refrigerator, grabbed the three apple-juice glasses his mother had left him, and poured them into the sink.

"Jacob, don't be sarcastic with me. How are you feeling?"

"Fine. A little tired. I had to turn the volume knob way up and it took a lot out of me."

"Jacob, don't make me come home and punch you in the nose. Are you feeling better? Say yes."

"Yes."

"I don't believe you. How many glasses of apple juice did you drink?"

"I finished off three."

"Good. Go back to sleep. I love you."

"I love you too, Ma."

He hung up the phone. The phone rang. He picked it up.

"I'm fine, Isaac," he said, and hung up.

Grabbing the Night Sky, he climbed up to Isaac's bunk. For the next three hours he crouched on his brother's mattress, map of the Night Sky on his knees, wetting the backs of tiny planets, moons, and hundreds of stars and sticking them in their places on the ceiling. Laughing to himself, he imagined Isaac's expression as he turned off his reading light and the Night Sky over Kansas exploded above.

That evening Isaac got into bed and, as usual, read for about an hour. Jacob knew Isaac was reading a novel about a boy who had overcome some horrible physical ailment to become an Olympic athlete. He knew because Isaac occasionally read aloud to him, though Jacob asked him not to. All Isaac ever read were books about athletes who had had to overcome horrible disabilities.

"Hey, Jacob, let me read you this."

"I'm tired, Isaac, and your light is keeping me awake."

"I'll turn it off. All you had to do was ask. You feeling well enough to go to school tomorrow?"

"I felt good enough to go today."

"Jacob, wake me if you have any problems breathing."

"Good night, Isaac."

"Good night, little brother. Sleep well."

The lights clicked off.

Silence. Jacob stared up into the thick, cloudy darkness that floated beneath Isaac's bunk. He waited. He wondered. Was Isaac mute with terror, or was he asleep?

Jacob gently scratched at the low ceiling made by the wooden slats supporting Isaac's bunk. No response. He got out of bed and climbed the ladder up to the top bunk.

Isaac was asleep. Jacob sat down at the foot of the bed, careful not to wake him. He drew his knees up to his chest and surveyed the Sky, which glowed quietly, almost distantly, above him. He listened to the strong, clear sound of Isaac's breathing.

Imagining himself as that boy in Kansas, out by himself at night in that vast wheat field, Jacob looked up and suddenly felt very much alone.

3

S o you had yourself a little extra vacation?" the school secretary asked, looking up from Jacob's papers.

Jacob nodded his head yes. It was ten thirty. He had just come from Dr. Grophy's office. He was almost two hours and ten days late for class. His germ had developed into bronchitis, sending him to the emergency room twice, once for a shot of epinephrine. His mother had suggested again that he consider the Special 10 class. Jacob had responded by threatening to become a drug dealer. He'd start with his asthma medicines.

"What were you doing? Traveling?" the secretary asked.

Jacob nodded his head yes and watched anxiously as she filled out his pink admissions slip. "I'm going into a regular class, right?" he asked.

"You're going into 401," she said

"I'll take him there!"

Jacob spun around to see a girl his own age with frizzy red hair and green eyes. She must have been there all along, watching. She could have been reading his records, all those comments about his asthma.

"Cynthia, you weren't sent here to be an office monitor," the secretary said. "You're being punished."

"Okay, Lottie. Then you take him there, and I'll answer the phones," she offered, smiling.

The three of them looked around the office. Except for a five-year-old asleep on a bench with his thumb in his mouth, there was nobody else there to take Jacob upstairs. He turned back to the secretary's desk. The secretary directed her attention from the sleeping five-year-old to Jacob's papers. She signed the pink slip. She slid his records back into his cumulative folder. Reluctantly she handed both the slip and the folder to the girl with the frizzy red hair.

"Now, Cynthia, don't get lost," she warned.

"Lottie, who do you think we are?" she asked, backing away, pulling Jacob by his arm. "Hansel and Gretel?"

Lottie sighed and returned to her papers. Cynthia laughed and led Jacob out of the office.

"You're funny," Jacob said as they climbed the stairs.

But she didn't hear him. She seemed lost in a song, as she danced her way up the stairs, still holding his arm. She was making him nervous. He stopped.

"What's 401 like?" he asked.

She stopped singing and turned to face him. She was wearing a white turtleneck and an oversize black vest. She put her hands on her hips and looked him up and down. She seemed pleased. "Did you know that Fred Astaire always wore a grey shirt because it looked like white in black-and-white movies?" she asked.

"No, I didn't," Jacob answered.

"You have on a grey shirt," she pointed out, "and you

17

keep your hands in your pockets. Fred Astaire kept his hands in his pockets when he wasn't dancing because he thought his hands were too big. You dance?"

"No."

"Too bad. You have a nice grey shirt. And I need a partner."

He didn't know what to say. He had never seen a girl with green eyes before. And frizzy red hair. And earrings with clock faces.

"C'mon," she said, and took him to his class.

She stopped him just outside of the room. "Here it is."

"Thanks."

"You've got Ms. Brace," she announced, tapping her right foot. She must have been wearing taps. The sound pinged through the hall. "She's pretty," she said, and gave him his pink slip and folder. "My name is Cynthia."

Suddenly his own name seemed awkward and clumsy. He couldn't say it. He looked down at his pink slip. PLEASE ADMIT ONE *Jacob Katz*, it read.

"My name is Jacob," he said. But it was too late. She was already too far down the hall, lost in another song.

He glanced back down at his record folder. There was a yellow piece of paper stuck to it. MEDICAL RE-MINDER: CHILD SEVERE ASTHMATIC, it read. He tore it off and stuck it into his back pocket. He glanced down the hallway. She was gone. He pushed open the door and stepped right into his teacher.

He looked up. His new teacher was very tall and sexy. She was wearing tight jeans and a baggy black blouse. She wore a silver string tie with a little blue armadillo for a clasp. She had short blond hair and peacock-feather earrings. She smiled and put her hand on Jacob's shoulder. Suddenly Jacob felt warm. The back of his collar itched. He offered her his pink slip and folder. He looked down at the floor.

She was wearing pointy cowboy boots.

"So you're Jacob Katz," she said cheerfully. "We've been waiting for you. Just a second."

She walked over to the front of the classroom and quickly wrote some math word-problems on the board.

"When you're finished with your essays, you can try these," she announced to the class, and then returned.

"This is a regular class, right?" Jacob asked.

"Yes, of course."

Yes! He had done it. He felt like applauding himself. Again Ms. Brace put her hand on his shoulder.

"Jacob, I just wanted to talk with you first," she said, guiding him towards the back of the classroom, by the closets. She knelt beside him. "How are you feeling?"

She had a wide, thin smile. She looked understanding. Too understanding. He glanced down at her tie clasp. He fought the urge to stare at her breasts. She reminded him of a painting in one of his mother's art books. A nude. He had snuck glances at it when he was home alone. She gently squeezed his shoulder.

"How are you feeling?" she asked again.

He turned to the problems on the board. Simple percentages and statistics.

"How is your asthma?" she asked. She sounded too concerned.

He looked over to the kids sitting nearest to them. They hadn't heard. They were busy writing.

"I can do those problems," he said.

"We've discussed it in class," she said. "How difficult life can be for a young person with asthma."

"I don't have asthma. Where can I sit? Can I sit over there?" he asked, pointing to an empty chair on the other side of the room, by the windows.

"I don't think there's anything to feel ashamed about," she tried to reassure him.

"I'm going to sit over there," Jacob said, and quickly made his way to the empty seat. He opened his loose leaf and began to copy down the problems. But the first problem didn't make any sense to him. He couldn't concentrate. Why had she told the class he had asthma? Why? He tried the problem.

Lavarr wanted to buy a cow. He saved up $150, which was 15% of its cost. How much more would he have to save?

"You need any help?" the boy next to him asked.

"No," he said. "I don't need any help. Lavarr needs help. Why the heck is he buying a cow? How's he going to get it home, anyway? Take the subway?"

The boy laughed. Then he asked Jacob how he was feeling.

"Fine, how are *you* feeling?" Jacob challenged him.

"Ms. Brace told us all about you and your asthma," the boy replied.

"She must have been talking about somebody else."

"Class, I'd like to have your attention, please," Ms. Brace said, sitting down on a girl's desk towards the front of the room.

"Hey, you guys choose up sides yet for baseball during recess?" Jacob whispered to the boy.

"Does anybody want to read their essays?" she asked.

Jacob looked around and noticed that quite a few of the kids in the class were looking at him.

"You can play baseball?" the boy next to him whispered.

"I'm a good second baseman," Jacob whispered back. "I can pivot really well. I've got quick hands."

"Nobody wants to read their essays?" Ms. Brace asked, looking defeated.

"What were the essays about?" Jacob asked the boy.

"How we would want our friends to treat us if we were disabled," the boy said.

This was horrible. What had she told them? Jacob raised his hand.

"Yes, Jacob?" Ms. Brace asked.

"I don't understand. . . . I don't understand the math problem."

"Well, we can discuss the math after the essays," Ms. Brace suggested.

"Why did she tell you I had asthma?" Jacob whispered to the boy. "Why did she tell you there was something wrong with me?"

"She wanted us all to understand you better. She said you were a special kid."

"I'll read my essay, Ms. Brace," a girl in the front called out.

"There's nothing special about me," Jacob told the boy.

"All right, Faleema. Please stand up when you read."

"I don't understand the math," Jacob insisted loudly.

Ms. Brace stood up. "That's all right, Jacob," she said, again in her understanding voice. "We can get to it later. Why don't you just listen to our essays. I think you might appreciate them. Maybe when they're done, you can even comment and offer us some advice." She turned to Faleema. "Please begin."

"But why is this kid buying a cow? That's all I want to know," Jacob insisted.

A few kids laughed. That felt good.

Ms. Brace smiled along with them.

"If I was disabled," Faleema began to read from her paper, "I would want my friends to understand how difficult it was for me to—"

"I mean, where is he going to park this cow?" Jacob demanded.

But this time nobody was laughing.

"Faleema, please continue," Ms. Brace said.

". . . how difficult it was for me to do some of the things they could do so easily. But I wouldn't want them to think I wasn't as good a person as they were . . ."

As Faleema read, Jacob tried not to listen. He took out his copy of *Legends of Crime* and, placing it on his lap, read about the James Gang.

When Faleema was finished, a small boy named Omar volunteered to read his essay.

"I'd feel bad, not being able to play sports. That's what boys do," Omar read.

Jacob struggled with Jesse and Frank terrorizing Union soldiers during the war. He had never really liked those two. He flipped to Bat Masterson.

After Omar read, the boy next to him raised his hand. Standing right above Jacob, he read, "I would want my friends to visit me in the hospital and bring me my comics and games," he said.

22

Jacob slipped his book into his backpack. He closed his loose leaf and raised his hand.

"Yes, Jacob?" Ms. Brace asked.

"I have to go to the bathroom," Jacob said.

Ms. Brace nodded her approval. Jacob stood up, grabbed his backpack, and made his way to the door.

"Why is he taking his backpack?" he heard someone ask.

"He's probably got his medicines in there," someone answered.

"Are you all right?" Ms. Brace whispered to him, stopping him at the door. "You look pale."

"I'm fine," Jacob said.

"Good. Then maybe when you come back you can give us your own thoughts," she suggested.

He looked up at her. He wanted to tell her he hated her, but he couldn't speak. There was something caught in his throat. He closed the door behind him and walked over to the water fountain. He drank until that sickly bubble in his throat disappeared. He looked up at the clock. It was a quarter to twelve. They would be going to lunch in fifteen minutes. *Now* who was going to pick him for their team? *Now* who would ever want him on their side?

He pushed open the doors to the stairs.

"Hey, where you off to?" It was the girl with the frizzy red hair.

He just waved and kept on walking. He couldn't answer her. He didn't know.

4

urning the corner onto Broadway, Jacob wondered where he could go. Home? How could he go back home? It was twelve o'clock. It was sunny and warm, and he was feeling pretty healthy. He had just spent the last ten days in bed. He couldn't go up to that apartment. It would be like walking back into prison. He sat down on a bench outside an ice-cream store and thought about where to go now.

Not back to school. Not back to that class. They all thought he was some sickly, helpless kid. They would all want to be nice to him. He shuddered. He looked at his hands. They were big hands. Like Fred Astaire's. Who was Fred Astaire? Who was that girl with the frizzy red hair? What class was she in? He stood up. He had to tell her not to listen to what anybody said about him. He started walking quickly back to the school.

He stopped. They would put him back into that class, he realized. Or they might even decide that he did belong in that Special 10 class. He stuck his hands back into his pockets and turned around. He continued walking down Broadway, away from the school. He just wanted to be somewhere nobody knew anything about him. Where there was nothing wrong with him.

But there wasn't anyplace to go.

Passing by a sporting-goods store, Jacob started thinking about Isaac. Right now he was probably surrounded by friends, doing something that involved sweating. Even though Isaac was a good student, Jacob could only picture his brother in gym, playing basketball, or outside, playing roller hockey. Jacob's only consolation was that Isaac wasn't much better than him at roller hockey. Isaac was too clean. He wasn't sneaky or aggressive enough to rid himself of the defense to get a clear shot.

Jacob loved roller hockey. Walking down Broadway toward his apartment, as if he were being pulled there, Jacob wished he was on his way to a game. For some reason roller hockey rarely triggered his asthma. Nor did he have Isaac's problem. Jacob was about as sneaky and aggressive as you could get. Often, by "accident," his stick would get stuck under the skates of his opponents. Also by "accident," he often skated full speed into his opponents, sending them flying into fences and sand boxes. If some guy from the other team came skating full speed at him, Jacob would suddenly remember to tie the laces on his skates, causing the boy to flip-flop over him. Jacob often scored two goals a game. But what he really liked about roller hockey were the fights.

First you called your opponent a vicious name. Then you threw down your gloves. Then you pushed him. He pushed you back. Then you grabbed his jersey and tried to pull it over his head. He tried to do the same to you. You both fell to the ground. Then the referee came and ordered you to go sit in the "penalty box," which was usually an infants' swing, over on the side. In the "penalty box" you could rest up a bit and continue to call the other guy horrible names. Sometimes, when you were really mad, or your team needed a boost, you called his mother and sister names too. But you didn't stand up or leave that box. Maybe, if you really needed to look fierce, you leaned forward, but you didn't get carried away. Jacob was always aware that he was short and skinny, and usually much younger than the other players. That other guy could always beat him up after the game. That's why he loved hockey fights. They let you look tough without getting hurt or losing your breath.

Isaac didn't enjoy hockey fights. He didn't like fights of any kind. He was a coward, but he was an odd coward. He was so afraid of the possibility of getting into a fight that if some boy pushed or threatened him, Isaac immediately punched him in the nose. He was so afraid of fighting, he needed to get it over with as quickly as possible.

It worked. Unlike Jacob, Isaac was strong. Any boy Isaac punched in the nose wanted to lie down for a while to think about things. Even if Jacob knelt beside the boy and informed him of Isaac's terrible fear of fighting, that boy rarely showed any desire to stand up and resume what he had started. Watching Isaac regain his happy composure as the prospect of a fight diminished, Jacob would become more and more angry. He would implore the boy to stand up and fight.

"Can't you see he's afraid of you?" Jacob would yell at the boy.

"I'm sorry. Are you all right?" Isaac would ask the boy

he had just punched. Isaac didn't want to encourage bad feelings. A grudge might lead to another fight. After he was satisfied that the boy forgave him, Isaac would leave. This would infuriate Jacob.

"Coward! What are you afraid of?" he would shout at Isaac.

"Shh! Let him go," the boy on the floor would plead.

"Let him go? What are you talking about?" Jacob would yell at the boy. "Can't you see he's afraid of you? Look at him walking away. He's a coward. Can't you see? He only hit you like that 'cause he's afraid of you."

"Is my nose bleeding? I think it's bleeding. Do you think he broke it?"

"Listen. You really scared him. Get up," Jacob would urge.

"Is he gone yet?" the boy would ask.

"No. I can still see him. I think he's trying to get away. If you hurry up, you can catch him."

Jacob would offer the boy his hand. The boy would delicately touch the bridge of his nose and wince. "You sure it's not broken?"

Jacob would kick the dirt, swear, then walk away, defeated. His brother had won again. Isaac never lost. It wasn't fair. Isaac couldn't be knocked down. Maybe it was because nobody but Jacob knew about Isaac's fears.

Fights! Not only was he afraid of getting into fights, he couldn't be in the same room as one. Watching westerns, he turned off the set as soon as the heroes rolled up their sleeves or pulled out their guns. He covered his ears when their mother yelled at him. If he passed by kids arguing over some candy, Isaac would stop and try to negotiate a settlement. If the kids were so young they hadn't learned to speak yet, he would patiently try to teach them how to say please and no thanks.

But it was more than just fights. Ever since their father had begun touring, almost three years ago, Isaac had begun developing these odd fears. Some made sense to Jacob; some didn't. Isaac was afraid of a comet striking New York. He was afraid of a nuclear accident. These made sense to Jacob. But Isaac was equally afraid that he would be walking by a phone booth and the phone would ring, and he would be forced to answer it. Isaac crossed the street to avoid vacant phone booths. He lived in Manhattan, yet he spent time worrying about poisonous jelly fish. The idea of infinity frightened him.

Isaac was also afraid when Jacob had an asthma attack. Why? What did Isaac think was going to happen? Jacob couldn't stand it. He wanted to find some place where nobody was worried about him.

Passing the kiosk of the blind newspaper dealer, Jacob stopped. The dealer, an elderly, drawn-faced man with wispy grey hair and clear blue eyes, appeared to be lost in a dream. Holding a small transistor radio, he was listening to classical music and gazing out onto the street through his tiny open window. Something about the dealer bothered Jacob, struck him as false.

He wasn't wearing sunglasses. He didn't look blind. Jacob thought the dealer was trying to get away with something.

"Hey, how come you don't wear sunglasses?" Jacob asked. It was more of a challenge than a question.

The dealer turned off his radio and looked past Jacob. He smiled. "Why? Is it sunny out?" he asked.

28

"No. You know what I mean. Like Stevie Wonder or Ray Charles."

"Maybe I don't play the piano," the dealer laughed.

Frustrated by the teasing, Jacob couldn't say what he wanted to say. He couldn't say the word "blind." It sounded too much like an insult. "You know. Like Stevie Wonder."

"Maybe I got a different sense of fashion. How come you're so concerned?"

"Because last week you said I didn't have to feel sorry for you. You don't wear sunglasses because you don't want people to feel sorry for you."

"If you wear sunglasses, people feel sorry for you?" the dealer asked. "Is that what happens to you, kid? When you wear sunglasses, people feel sorry for you?"

"No. People feel sorry for me all the time. Which is stupid. I don't want them to. I'm fine. I don't need it. Isaac needs it more than I do."

"Yeah? Who's Isaac?"

"Isaac's my older brother. And nobody feels sorry for him, although they should. He's crazy. Nothing bad can ever happen to him. Nothing's wrong with him, but he still has all of these crazy fears. Like fighting. But no fight lasts longer than one of his punches. And quicksand. He's terrified he's going to step into the stuff and disappear."

"Quicksand?" the dealer asked, amused.

"Quicksand!" Jacob yelled back. "Quicksand! In Manhattan! I always say to him, 'Where, Isaac? Where? Show me!' "

The dealer laughed. An elderly woman came by and picked up a paper. She dropped some change onto the ledge of the dealer's window and walked away.

"He's afraid of scorpions," Jacob said.

"Isaac?" the dealer asked.

"Yes, Isaac. Before we were going to sleep once, he said, 'Wait. What if one just dropped onto my bed when I was sleeping?'

"I said, 'What, Isaac? If what just dropped onto your bed?'

"And he said, 'A scorpion.' "

"They're very dangerous, scorpions," the dealer said.

"What? What scorpion? How's a scorpion going to drop onto his bed? How's it going to get to Manhattan. How's it going to get to the Upper West Side? How's it going to get up five flights of steps? How's it going to drop onto his bed? He has the top bunk. The only way a scorpion's going to drop onto his bed is if I throw it up there."

"Did you explain this to him?"

"Yes. I said, 'The only way a scorpion's going to drop onto your bed, Isaac, is if I throw it up there.'

"And he said, 'You wouldn't ever do that, right?' "

"And what did you say?" the dealer asked, smiling.

"I didn't say anything."

The two of them laughed.

Suddenly Jacob felt a hand on his shoulder. He spun around.

"Jacob Katz?" a police officer asked. "You the kid who's missing from P.S. 89?"

5

oes my mother know?" Jacob asked, sliding into the backseat of the police car.

"I don't know, kid," the officer said. "All I know is I'm supposed to return this asthmatic kid, name, Jacob Katz, who fits your description, back to P.S. 89."

Not only did his class know, but now the entire Police Department of New York City knew he had asthma. Hearing it from a cop's mouth, however, made it sound more like a crime. Jacob liked that.

But he couldn't enjoy the ride back to school in the police car not knowing whether his mother had been called. If she had, she would panic. She would also be considering that Special 10 class. "They're in the same situation you are in, Jacob," she would say. "They don't need to be taught how to be your friend."

As Jacob waited with the policeman outside of the principal's office, the girl with the frizzy red hair and green eyes entered, carrying an armful of paintings. Singing to herself, she walked right past him and dropped the paintings onto the school secretary's desk.

"Hi," Jacob said.

She turned, smiled, then noticed the policeman. She seemed amused.

"I thought you'd never let them bring you back alive," she said.

Jacob shrugged his shoulders. She talked to him as if he were a character in a movie, a dancer, a mobster. She certainly didn't feel sorry for him.

"Jacob, please come in." It was the principal.

Jacob stepped into his office.

"Thank you, officer." The principal shook the policeman's hand, then closed the door behind them. "Jacob, please take a seat."

"Did you call my mother?" Jacob asked two steps into the room.

"No. We couldn't get in contact with her. You had five numbers on your record card, but three were for theaters that hadn't opened yet and two were for bookstores where your mother no longer worked."

That made sense. His mother had just begun working in the rare-books department of the Argosy. She had given him three copies of the store's phone number to bring to school: one for his teacher, one for the office, and one for himself. All three were still in his pocket. He felt tremendously relieved.

"Jacob, I don't believe we've met. I'm Mr. Macombo." He offered Jacob his hand. Jacob looked up at Mr. Macombo, a tall, thin man, about his father's age, balding, with round, wire-framed glasses. He looked past him and saw autographed photos of Mr. Macombo with Big Bird and the Incredible Hulk.

"I'm not going back to that class," he said.

"Please sit down," Mr. Macombo said.

Jacob sat down in a big overstuffed leather chair. Mr. Macombo pulled up a chair right next to Jacob. He crossed his legs, folded his hands on his lap, and smiled. Jacob read the smile as saying, "I'll wait. This is a troubled child. I'll be patient."

"I'm not a troubled child," Jacob said, answering the smile. "Isaac is. I'm not."

"Who is Isaac?"

"He's my brother, and he's afraid of falling into quicksand. You should call his principal, and his teachers and his guidance counselor. He goes to Junior High 78. The other kids in his classes should probably know about him. He's a very nervous kid, even though he always looks happy, and he skates well. Maybe each of his teachers should make an announcement about him to their classes. You want his school's phone number?" Jacob reached into his back pocket for his wallet and Isaac's phone number.

Mr. Macombo continued to smile. He wasn't going to call Isaac's principal.

"I'm not going back to that class."

"Jacob, Ms. Brace is a very fine teacher."

"She warned the kids about me. She warned them."

"She didn't warn them, Jacob. She tried to make them sensitive to your needs. It was at my suggestion. I consider P.S. 89 to be one large family. We're all very concerned about each other. We want you to think of us that way. Instead of running away from us, you should come to us when you have a problem."

"But I don't have a problem!" Jacob shouted. "And I don't need another family."

Mr. Macombo smiled.

"I'm not going back to that class, Mr. Macombo. Put me into another class and don't tell anybody about me. Just let me take care of myself."

"Jacob, you belong with the students in Ms. Brace's class."

"No, I don't. I belong with . . . What class is that office monitor in?"

"Cynthia?"

"The girl with the red hair."

"Cynthia," Mr. Macombo said, shaking his head in disapproval. "When she's not walking out of her class, she's with Ms. Pelham, our other sixth-grade teacher."

"Put me in that class."

"Jacob, you and Cynthia are two very different students. She has certain . . . needs, which you, I hope, will never have. We put you in Ms. Brace's class because she is a sensitive teacher, and because your reading scores are very high, and we group our children according to their reading scores. The other sixth-grade class has much lower reading scores. You would not fit in."

"So don't tell them about my scores."

"Jacob . . . you don't seem to understand. They're not as academically gifted as you are."

Mr. Macombo was saying something and was not saying something at the same time. He was trying to shake him off, using adult words to get around him.

"So I'll pretend I'm not smart," Jacob said. "That's all right with me. I'll be smart at home. The kids won't know. Put me in that class."

"Jacob . . ." Mr. Macombo's understanding smile was giving way to a look of frustration. "Your intellectual performance capabilities are much higher than those of the children in Ms. Pelham's class."

"They don't do well on tests? Fine. So I'll fail some tests. I can do that. It doesn't bother me. I'll just tell my mother

34

about it before I take one. I can take it over after school."

"Your written and verbal skills—"

"Verbal means talking, right? So I won't talk in class. I won't even raise my hand. If the teacher calls on me, I'll just give the wrong answer, or I'll say I wasn't paying attention. Put me in that class."

"Jacob . . ."

"Mr. Macombo, please. I can't go back to that other class. The kids think I'm diseased, or I'm dying or something. Please. Put me in Ms. Pelham's class. And don't tell her I have asthma. I don't. There's nothing wrong with me. I'm just a regular kid. I just want to have friends and be a regular kid."

Mr. Macombo stood up and went over to his desk. From the top of a stack of papers he picked up Jacob's record folder and removed a long yellow sheet. Jacob recognized the form. He suddenly felt queasy.

"How come your parents never signed the Special 10 class form?" Mr. Macombo asked, reading over his evaluation.

"Because it's only for sick kids. Really sick kids. I belong in Ms. Pelham's class."

"Why don't we try this," Mr. Macombo said, still reading. "We'll put you in Ms. Pelham's class, and if that doesn't work," he said, looking up, "maybe we should get your parents in here to reconsider the Special 10 class. It's a good program, Jacob. They eat lunch and have recess with the rest of the sixth-graders. And each year they put on a play about their own lives."

"I hate acting," Jacob said.

"It's really quite moving," Mr. Macombo said, and began to fill out a new pink admissions slip.

6

The kids in his new class were copying math problems from the board when Jacob entered the room. Some kids glanced up, but didn't show any interest when he handed Ms. Pelham the note Mr. Macombo had given him. He looked around the room for Cynthia. She had left the office before him. There was a girl seated behind a portable blackboard in the back. All he could see was her white skirt, skinny legs, and shiny shoes. He tried to remember what Cynthia had been wearing.

After putting on her bifocals and reading his note, Ms. Pelham looked up at him, shook her head disapprovingly, and told him to sit next to Wilkes.

"Who is Wilkes?" Jacob asked.

"Wilkes!" Ms. Pelham shouted.

"What? I didn't do nothing!" a boy in the back called out.

"That's Wilkes," Ms. Pelham said, frowning.

Wilkes was a stocky kid with curly black hair and thick black-rimmed glasses.

"Copy and answer the problems on the board," Ms. Pelham told Jacob.

He sat down behind his new desk, put away his books,

and got to work, watching Wilkes out of the corner of his eye. Wilkes attacked a problem, solved it quickly and accurately, but then immediately started to erase what he had written. He erased so desperately and thoroughly, he put a hole in his paper.

Wilkes made Jacob nervous. He tried to ignore him. He started on the problems on the board. They were all simple multiplication and division word-problems, much easier than what he had seen in Ms. Brace's class. He finished them in ten minutes. He looked around. The rest of the kids were still working. The boy to his right was about halfway through the twenty problems. The girl in front of him was up to the fifth. He snuck a glance at Wilkes. He was on his second problem. His pencil was almost down to its nub. He had erased three holes in his paper.

What now? It would soon be three o'clock. Then he could at least get another glance at Cynthia. Or maybe get himself into a baseball game with the kids in his new class. He considered reading, but he didn't want Wilkes to know he had finished the work. He didn't want anybody to know he didn't belong there, that he was any different from them. And he didn't want Wilkes to feel bad. He thought of helping him, but the class was so quiet, Ms. Pelham would hear him if he even whispered. He rechecked his work. He started to doodle. He drew a sports car chasing other sports cars. He drew clouds of dust spewing out from under the wheels. He noticed Wilkes had stopped working.

Wilkes was staring at his own hands. He seemed confused. He turned them over, examining the palms, then the backs. He rubbed them together, brought each palm to his nose, sniffed, then rested them on the desk. He began to tap his fingers, one at a time, as if testing them.

"No," Wilkes mumbled to himself.

Something was wrong. Again he brought his palms up to his nose. He inhaled deeply. This seemed to upset him further. He began to sniff each finger. Again he shook his head and mumbled, "No."

He caught Jacob watching him, blushed, and quickly stuck his hands into his desk.

"I think I have an emergency," Wilkes confided to Jacob.

"What's the matter?" Jacob whispered. "Are you all right?"

"My hands," Wilkes whispered, looking around, embarrassed. "My hands."

"What's the matter with them?"

Wilkes looked around to see if anybody else was listening. They weren't. He smiled apologetically at Jacob. "My hands . . . they smell funny."

Jacob knew that this would be a good time to change the subject, to talk about math, the new school year, the Mets, or girls. He knew that it would also be a good time to return to his doodling or to review his work. He knew all of this, yet somehow he found himself responding.

"What do your hands smell like?" he asked.

"They don't smell like my hands," Wilkes confessed.

Jacob looked down at the sports cars on his paper for help. Maybe he could borrow one of them and drive right out of there. Mr. Macombo had said the kids in his new class hadn't done well on their test scores. What sort of tests had he been talking about? Maybe if he looked at his sports cars long enough, Wilkes would forget about him. He began to pray silently that Wilkes would not ask him to smell his hands. He prayed that Wilkes wouldn't ask him to decide to whom those hands really belonged. Whose hands did he think he had?

"They don't smell like my hands," Wilkes reminded him.

"Shh," Jacob whispered. "It's nothing. You probably have a cold. You probably just can't smell right."

"My nose doesn't smell like my nose?" Wilkes asked. He looked shattered.

Bad things were about to happen. The kid next to him was not sure his own fingers belonged to him. A kid like that was a dangerous kid to sit next to, especially when that kid suspected you knew something about his nose you weren't willing to admit.

Wilkes began to snicker. He rested his chin on his desk and shoved his hands inside.

Jacob looked down at his sports cars. Maybe he could draw Wilkes into one of them, then erase him.

"I don't smell them now," he whispered to Jacob. "I'll just keep them inside my desk."

"Good idea," Jacob said, looking away.

"I'm not going to think about them anymore," Wilkes said.

"Good idea," Jacob said, drawing another sports car. He left its passenger seat empty for Wilkes.

"They do smell funny," Wilkes insisted.

"Just keep them inside your desk," Jacob suggested.

"You can smell them too?"

"No. No, I can't smell them at all."

"No? Here, smell them."

Jacob leapt backwards to avoid Wilkes's hands. The next thing he knew, he was on the floor, twisted, his desk, books, and Wilkes on top of him. Wilkes was punching him in the back and shouting, "I didn't do nothing! I didn't do nothing!"

"Stop hitting me, Wilkes!"

"Get up, you two," Ms. Pelham demanded.

Wilkes pounded him on the back.

Jacob lost his breath.

"I said, get up!" Ms. Pelham shouted.

"I didn't do nothing!" Wilkes shouted back.

Taking in as deep a breath as he could, Jacob yanked his foot out of his sneaker, spun around, and belted Wilkes in the nose.

Wilkes began to wail.

Jacob tried to catch his breath. He had begun to wheeze. Gasping for air, he stood up, righted his desk, and picked up his books. He put his sneaker back on.

Holding his nose, Wilkes continued to wail.

Jacob opened up his loose leaf and turned to his math work. He tried to write, but his wheezing was getting worse.

"You all right?" somebody asked, putting a hand on his shoulder. He looked up. It was Cynthia.

"Yes" was all he could say.

She was going to watch him get a bad attack. He leaned forward and dug his fists into his thighs, and tried to blow out the thick, salty air that was stuck in his chest. He wanted to be able to speak, to tell her, to tell the whole class, that nothing was wrong with him, to forget it, to go away. He could take care of himself.

Suddenly he realized a crowd had gathered around him. They were curious and frightened, watching him struggle for air. Did they think they were watching him die? He had to stand. He would go into the hallway, hide someplace, and take his spray. He'd come back as if nothing had happened. He pushed himself up from his desk.

"And where do you think you're going?" Ms. Pelham asked, standing over him.

"I didn't do nothing!" Wilkes cried out, pushing his way through the crowd to Ms. Pelham. "I didn't do nothing!" He tugged on Ms. Pelham's sleeve.

"Oh, Wilkes," Cynthia said, "shut up. Just go pick up your desk and be quiet."

Wilkes did as he was told.

Jacob took a few steps towards the door. "I'll be right back," he was able to say, but then he had to stop to breathe. He leaned forward and, pushing his hands against the back of a chair, tried to suck in as much air as he could.

"I said, where do you think you're going?" Ms. Pelham repeated.

"I don't think he feels too good, Ms. Pelham," Cynthia said.

"Cynthia!" Ms. Pelham shouted.

He stood up straight. He wasn't going to take any medicine in front of all of these kids.

"I'll be right back," he said to Ms. Pelham.

Ms. Pelham grabbed him by the shoulder. Her nails dug into his skin. "You're not going anywhere until you explain—"

"Ms. Pelham," Cynthia interrupted. "I don't—"

"Cynthia!" Ms. Pelham shouted.

"Pelham!" Cynthia shouted back. "I don't think he feels too good. Let me take him to the nurse."

"Cynthia, you will take him to the office," Ms. Pelham said calmly. "And you will give Mr. Macombo this note."

Jacob took a few steps forward and leaned against the

door. His windpipe was as constricted as a straw. He wasn't getting enough air. He watched Ms. Pelham walk over to her desk and quickly scribble something on a long yellow sheet. Cynthia waited with her hands on her hips, tapping her right foot. The metal studs snapped against the floor like shots.

Ms. Pelham handed her the note. "You will take him to the office and give this to Mr. Macombo," she said. "And I will call your home tonight before dinner."

"Don't ruin my appetite," Cynthia mumbled just loudly enough for the whole class to hear.

The two of them left the classroom to the sound of laughter. "Sit down! All of you!" Ms. Pelham shouted, and slammed the door.

"You going to be all right? Can I help you?" Cynthia asked, smiling.

"Don't feel sorry for me," Jacob said as they entered the stairwell.

"Why should I feel sorry for you? I'm in as much trouble as you are."

Jacob sat down on a step. He took his spray. He held his breath.

"That your medicine?" she asked.

Jacob nodded his head yes and took the note from her.

Dear Mr. Macombo, it read. *I already have thirty-four children in my class. This child is a fighter, and is disrespectful. If you insist on placing him in my class, I will bring the matter up with the union.*

Jacob exhaled. She was kicking him out of her class. They were going to put him into that Special 10 class. They were going to make him into a "special" kid. He looked up at Cynthia. He had never seen eyes that pretty. He took his spray again.

"That was a funny line I said, wasn't it?" she asked. "Don't ruin my appetite." She laughed. "I always do that. It's from watching too many movies. I always say something 'cause it's funny. Then I get in trouble for saying it. And anyway, she can't call me. Our phone's been disconnected."

"You have pretty eyes," Jacob said, surprising himself.

"Thank you."

"I'm not going to this school anymore," he said, standing up. His lungs had cleared. "Thanks." He shook her hand.

"Hey, where you going?"

He didn't answer her. He wanted to ask her to come with him, and he thought she'd come if he asked. But he didn't want to get her in anymore trouble.

"Hey, where you going?"

Jacob couldn't bring himself to answer her. He was going where nobody felt sorry for him, where he wasn't special. He knew somebody else who needed a partner.

7

Spotting the newspaper dealer's kiosk down the block, Jacob stopped. He had almost been running. He wiped his nose on his sleeve and looked back up Broadway towards his school. He wanted to run back to Cynthia. He wanted to tell her something, but he didn't know what he wanted to say: That there was nothing wrong with him? That it felt good just to sit next to her on the stairs and look at her eyes and listen to her talk? That he wished he could dance?

But it didn't matter now, because he wasn't going back to that school. Ever. He turned and started walking towards the kiosk. When he reached it, he stood there quietly as the dealer spoke with a young woman about opera, about how good the Metropolitan once was. Jacob waited. He looked up and down the avenue, at the people walking past him, at the old women pushing shopping carts, at two joggers trotting by, at a ragged young drunk sitting on the ground, half asleep against the walls of a church.

He felt horrible inside. He was too alone. And what tore at him, even more than not being able to go back to that school and sit down in a regular class, was the frustration of not being able to control his own life. His asthma would always take over, bully him. No matter how badly he wanted something, no matter how hard he tried to get it, his asthma would always rise up and slap it away from him.

The young woman purchased a copy of the *Opera News* and left humming. The dealer turned on his radio.

"I'm back," Jacob announced.

The dealer turned off his radio. He looked confused.

"The kid with the crazy older brother," Jacob added.

"The kid with the police escort," the dealer laughed. "Well, Dillinger, you escape or you out on parole?"

"I escaped," Jacob said, delighted with the dealer's response. He seemed pleased that Jacob had returned. "They put me next to a kid who didn't think his hands were his hands. I'm not going back."

"Sounds reasonable. But what about when the police come for you again?"

"You'll tell them I'm working for you, that I'm your assistant," Jacob said, proud of his own cleverness. "That makes sense. I could stand here and make sure nobody steals your papers. And when nobody's around, I could read to you. I read really well."

"I'm sure you do, Dillinger," the dealer said. "And I'd appreciate having you around, but . . ."

"It would be like we were partners. Only I would really be working for you. You wouldn't even have to pay me that much."

"And I could lose my license," the dealer said, shaking his head. "Listen, Dillinger, you want to come around here after school and read to me, that would be great. I'd also

45

like to hear more stories about your crazy brother. But after school. Now you go back there before you get in trouble."

"I can't," Jacob said. "They're going to put me into a special class where everybody's got something wrong with them. I can't go into a class like that. Let me stay here. There's nowhere else for me to go."

"After school."

"C'mon. You need me. You're blind."

"That's right. Even without the sunglasses."

"I'm sorry," Jacob said.

"Don't apologize. Get going. Back to school. Now."

"Theodore, this kid bothering you?" a tall man in a dark suit asked the dealer.

Jacob didn't wait to hear the dealer's answer. He was already running.

He reached his building and sat down on the steps. He was wheezing again. He took his spray and held his breath. What was happening? His first day of school and he was back at home. He felt defeated, lost. Where could he go? He pictured Cynthia, sitting on the steps. He wished she could be sitting next to him. He wanted to hear her say something funny again, something that would get her into trouble. He exhaled slowly.

His heart was skittering. He had taken his spray too frequently in too short a time. He could breathe, but his hands were trembling. Even his medicine turned against him.

He stood up and reached into his back pockets for his keys. His keys weren't in his back pockets. He patted his other pockets. No keys.

"This is Isaac's fault," he told himself. He knew why

these things were happening to him. It was so they couldn't happen to Isaac. Jacob wondered why God had given him asthma and left Isaac alone. Isaac was probably in school right now, playing ball. Isaac, with those crazy fears he gave himself. Jacob pulled his pockets out of his pants. Pretzel crumbs and crumpled tissues fell to the ground, but no keys.

"No! No! No!" he shouted, and stamped his foot.

He stuck his hand into his jacket pocket. He felt the tip of his key chain. It had half fallen through the pocket into the lining of the jacket. He could barely get his index finger into the hole of the key ring. He yanked it. His keys went flying into the air. Helplessly he watched them bounce high off the pavement and skip merrily along towards a sewer grating.

"God is not a practical joker," he called to the keys. It was something he had heard his mom say. The keys skipped to the edge of the curb.

"Stop!"

The keys stopped bouncing. They lay flat on their side, their ragged tips overhanging the curb. Jacob felt proud of himself and his newly acquired power over keys.

"You wouldn't have listened to Isaac, would you?" he asked the keys as he picked them up. The keys glinted in his palm. "Then again, you probably wouldn't have run away from Isaac in the first place."

But why? Why was God so good to Isaac? Sure, Isaac had his crazy fears, his scorpions and quicksand, but he could always stay away from what threatened him. Jacob wished he could reverse the situation.

Quicksand. Scorpions. Jacob went through a list of Isaac's phobias. Fighting. Comets. Nuclear accidents.

Phone booths. Pirates. Isaac hadn't mentioned pirates lately. Pirates!

Jacob bounded up the stairs. He had thought of the perfect prank. It was unexpected. It didn't make sense. It was funny. Maybe it would even things out between the two of them.

"Yo ho ho and a bottle of rum!" Jacob sang as he climbed the last flight of stairs.

His mother opened the door as soon as he reached the landing.

"Ma?"

"Jacob? Oh, there you are. I was just going to your school, and I realized I wasn't even sure where it was. I was at rehearsal when your father registered you. Isaac called your school just to check up on you. They couldn't find you. Then they said you had snuck out of the building. What happened?"

"Ma, is Isaac still afraid of pirates?"

"No, I don't think so. I think he outgrew that fear a few years ago. Jacob, what happened?"

The phone rang. She picked it up.

"Yes . . . just a second." She handed him the phone. "It's Cynthia."

"Hello?"

"So anyway, so how are you?" she asked.

"I'm fine. There's nothing wrong with me," he said.

"Well, you can't dance. That's something."

"How did you get my number?" Jacob asked.

"I'm in the office. I looked it up. My social worker's here. She's in with Macombo. I think he's going to suspend me for the week."

"How come?"

"He gave me a long list of reasons, but I forgot to write them down. Also, he was mad I helped you escape. When they went looking for you, I told them you were hiding backstage in the auditorium. They looked. They weren't amused. So I'm going on vacation. You coming back to school?"

Jacob looked at his mother. Her arms were folded. She was growing impatient.

"No," he said.

"So then maybe I'll see you one of these days. I'll stop by. Oh, here they come. Gotta dance. Bye!"

She hung up.

"Jacob, what's going on?" his mother asked.

"I'm not going back to that school."

"What happened?"

"And I'm not going into any special class. Anywhere."

"Who was that on the phone?" she asked.

He didn't answer her, but went into his room and closed the door.

Tuesday morning was cool and cloudless, the beginning of another beautiful September day, and to Jacob, everybody along Broadway, kids and adults alike, seemed eager to get where they were going.

"I want to be suspended!" Jacob shouted at his mother, who was walking ahead of him. "I'm never going back!" Not to Ms. Brace's class. "I don't need to be understood!" he declared to the crowd, sounding like a politician at a rally. "There's no place for me there!" Those kids in Ms. Pelham's class had seen him have an attack. Now they would just wait for the next one, wait for him to come to school with tubes attached to his arms, a respirator strapped to his mouth. He stomped his feet, shook his hands. His mother was already a half block ahead of him. "I want to stay home!"

Cynthia was stopping by. That's what she had said. She could stop by any day. He had to be there when she came.

His mother appeared to be picking up her pace. He shouted at her. "They're all nut cases in that school! The kid I was sitting next to didn't even know if he had come to school with his own hands!" He ran over to the curb and kicked a parked car.

"Jacob, leave that car alone," his mother ordered. Though she hadn't shouted, her voice traveled well. It seemed to have more authority than any of the other street sounds. "Jacob, you are not staying home. We are going to talk with your principal, and we are going to get you back into class."

"What class?" he demanded to know. "I don't belong in any class."

"Stop that. Let's go. We have an appointment."

"But I don't want to talk to him. I want to be suspended. For life!" He ran over to an overstuffed garbage can and kicked it, spilling plastic bottles and trash onto the sidewalk. He stopped to pick it all up. "I don't mind staying home. I'll learn more," he told himself. "Isaac goes to school every day, and what does he learn? He learns to read stupid books about sick kids who become Olympic athletes. And he still calls rabbits 'bunnies'!"

His mother crossed 94th Street and continued uptown. He quickly stuffed the rest of the garbage back into the can. He had to sprint to catch up to her. He tugged on her sleeve.

"Ma, they should be suspending me. I got into a fight. I ran out of class. Twice! If they don't suspend me, I won't learn my lesson. And if you get them to put me back into Ms. Pelham's class, I'm going to become dumb, crazy, and boring, just like Isaac."

She continued walking.

"Then you're going to have two children who are failures. Everybody's going to think you're a bad parent."

"I never heard of anybody being called a bad parent because she put her child back into school," a man standing next to Jacob said.

51

He looked up. The man was tall, grey bearded with a round face. He had tiny blue eyes that disappeared when he smiled.

"There's a kid in my class," Jacob explained to the man, "this kid I sit next to, who doesn't think his hands are his hands."

The man shook his head and said, "Well, well."

"I deserve to be suspended," Jacob went on. "Cynthia's getting suspended just for helping me. And she . . ." Jacob pointed accusingly at his mother, who was now nearly a block in front, still walking determinedly ahead. "She wants to straighten everything out! What is she going to do?" he asked the man. "Put me back into Ms. Brace's class? The boys will pick me last for their teams. The girls will pretend to be extra nice to me and treat me like I'm going to die tomorrow. And then I'll feel like I *am* going to die tomorrow. And every time I miss a day of school the teacher's going to make everybody in the class write me get-well cards."

Jacob noticed his companion had stopped smiling. He seemed to be looking in the direction of Jacob's mother, who was stopped at a light a block ahead. Jacob assumed the man was wondering why a mother would do something to harm her own child. Jacob decided to enlist his help. They reached the curb and waited for the traffic to pass.

"I'm not going into any Special 10 class," he told the man. "Then the whole school feels sorry for you. And everybody thinks you're breakable."

"That must be unpleasant," the grey-bearded man said, looking straight ahead.

"And Cynthia, she wants me to be her partner. I don't

52

even know why, but she does. But she's not going to want to talk to me if I'm a Special 10 kid."

"Oh," the man said.

"Isaac! The only kid who will want to be my friend will be Isaac."

"Isaac?"

"He's my older brother," Jacob sadly admitted.

"Oh . . . well. . . . It must be good to have an older brother," the man said as the light changed. "You can talk to your older brother," he said, picking up the pace.

"Talk to Isaac? He's crazy!" Jacob said, also picking up the pace. "He's so strange. He's afraid of crazy things. He's afraid—he was afraid of being kidnapped by pirates. He's afraid of walking by open windows. He's afraid of rock music. He's afraid— Do you know what else he's afraid of?" Jacob laughed. "Dubbed movies! He won't watch Godzilla movies because he's afraid he's going to start talking like one of those scientists in the movies. You know—when you see them move their mouths, and no words come out, then a minute later you hear, 'We must stop Godzilla!' Isaac's afraid that's going to happen to him. He's afraid he's going to be dubbed. Like it's some kind of disease you can catch. Diseases! He's afraid that I'm going to die when he's asleep, and when he wakes up, he'll realize he could have saved my life. He's not good to talk to. He's crazy. And he feels sorry for me. You believe it?"

Jacob suddenly realized that while he was walking very quickly, he was still falling behind the man, who was now taking Paul Bunyon strides while staring straight ahead. Jacob understood. The man wanted him to disappear. He thought Jacob was crazy. He was trying to get away.

Jacob jogged up to the man.

"You haven't been listening to me," he told the man.

The man pretended not to hear him and began to race-walk.

"You know what I'm going to do?" Jacob declared as he jogged alongside him. "I'm going to run up to my mother. That's my mother over up there, up the block. And I'm going to tell her that you offered me ten bucks if I would come home with you. Ma! Ma!"

The grey-bearded man stopped walking. He gazed down at Jacob, his eyes wide open, showing his surprise and horror. Jacob returned the gaze with his cutest, innocent-boy smile.

"Ma! Ma!" Jacob sprinted up the avenue to his mother. Once he reached her, he had to stop and take his spray.

"You know I really should be suspended," he reminded her. "They really shouldn't let me back into that school. I really shouldn't go to school anymore. Maybe I should stay home and watch all of those educational programs on Channel Thirteen. I could learn to speak French. I could learn physics. I could learn how to fix our toilet."

She didn't hear him. She was listening to her own thoughts. Turning her worried look away from him, she shaded her eyes and peered into the distance uptown.

He was still wheezing. He took his spray and held his breath. Now, waiting for the medicine to take effect, watching everybody else on the avenue hurrying along, Jacob wondered how he could stop everything. Cynthia was coming to see him. He was not going back to school. He had to stop his mother from seeing Macombo and getting him back into that school. After everything that had happened, the Special 10 class was probably his only option.

He couldn't let it happen. He couldn't let his mother speak to Mr. Macombo. But what could he do?

Suddenly, he knew the answer—he would give in!

He would take his mother to see the principal. He just wouldn't take her to see *his* principal.

It might work. When they had moved to the Upper West Side, his mother and father had spent two weeks shopping for a school for him. But it was his father who had finally brought him to Mr. Macombo's school to be registered. Maybe his mother didn't remember which one they had finally picked. There were three or four schools right near each other. If he just walked up the stairs to a different one, maybe she wouldn't notice. He doubted she would stop to check the school's number or name.

What about the principal? She didn't have anything written down. Macombo's secretary had called his home. Would his mother remember the name Macombo? Possibly. Still, it was worth the risk. And if it didn't work, if he got caught, maybe Macombo would suspend him. Either way, he couldn't lose.

Putting on a bit of a show, Jacob grudgingly stood up and began walking uptown. He turned right on 96th Street.

"I thought you said it was on West End Avenue, Jacob," his mother said.

"Columbus, Ma. Columbus and 97th Street."

"Oh."

Yes! That "Oh" announced to Jacob that there was something else working in his favor: The Trance. It was a place her mind visited whenever she was focusing on learning a role she was about to play. She was now rehearsing what she was going to say to Mr. Macombo. She was in The Trance, a place far from the real world. Except for the word "asthma," sounds usually took twenty to thirty minutes to reach her when she was in The Trance. Jacob had often used The Trance to entertain himself. In the hours before her opening nights, he would sit down next to her and count the number of "Oh's" his mother emitted in response to a series of outrageous statements.

"Ma, Isaac and I have decided to marry each other."

"Oh."

"We had to. Isaac's pregnant."

"Oh."

"So we're going to Mars."

"Oh."

"We're taking Dad's spaceship."

"Oh."

"But first we have to put on your clothes and cover our bodies in catsup and vanilla ice cream."

"Oh."

The record for "oh's" stood at twenty-three. Maybe today it would be beaten.

With his mother in Trance Land, Jacob led her to a school that looked just like his own school, except it wasn't. He walked up the steps to the side entrance, opened a door, walked down a short flight of steps, opened another door marked OFFICE, and bumped right into a short, fat, unshaven man in brown overalls. Jacob read the badge on the man's breast pocket: FERNANDO LINCOLN, *Custodian*. Jacob asked directions to the principal's office.

"Up the stairs and to the right."

Jacob led the way. His mother followed, showing not

the least bit of curiosity as to why they had visited the boiler room first. She was still in The Trance. Jacob found the Main Office and entered. It was a large room divided by a shoulder-high counter. The artwork of children was all over the walls, though there were no kids around. Only a bald, chubby man, speaking on the phone.

On the counter directly in front of Jacob was a sign-in book and a small box containing discount coupons for plays around New York. Waiting for the phone call to end, Jacob began to rummage through the coupons. His father had unsuccessfully auditioned for most of the plays in the box. He missed his father. He resented the plays listed on the coupons for rejecting him, for sending him away to Chicago. He looked through the box for a coupon to his mother's theater. There weren't any. Probably because it didn't cost more than five dollars to see one of his mother's shows. Sometimes the plays were so odd, the director would give away free apple cider and cookies to anyone who promised to sit through the first act. But at least there could have been a little slip mentioning the name of the theater. He began to resent the school.

"I hate this school," he told his mother. "I won't mind it when they suspend me."

"May I help you?" the bald man asked, putting down the phone.

"Yes. My mother would like to speak with . . . with Principal . . ." Jacob pretended to have forgotten the principal's name, hoping the man would supply it.

"Principal . . ." Jacob mumbled. "Principal . . . Mr. . . . ."

"Mrs. Kaufman, the principal?" the man asked. "Perhaps I can help you. I'm her secretary."

"Escape! Flee!" a voice inside Jacob's head screamed.

"Duck for cover!" Mr. Macombo had just become a lady. The female secretary who had called his home had just become a guy. Different school, different principal, different sexes. Inside his head Jacob heard the sound of bugles and a voice call, "Retreat!"

His mother smiled politely and nodded her head. She was still in The Trance! Hope. She was probably waiting for her cue to start her performance.

"Is this about registering your child?"

"No! It wasn't my fault!" Jacob shouted, and kicked the floor. "It wasn't my fault!"

"I'm here about my child's—"

"Suspension!" Jacob interjected. "Permanent suspension," he said, hoping to sound disgusted. "Suspension for life."

His mother looked down at him, blinked, then rubbed her eyes. "Jacob?" she asked.

She was coming out of The Trance. He had to act quickly.

The secretary turned to his mother. "And your child's name is—"

"Trouble!" Jacob cried. "How come I got into trouble? It wasn't my fault!" He glared down at the bin of theater coupons. "I hate this school!" He slammed his fist down onto the edge of the bin. The coupons flew into the air.

"Young man!"

"Jacob!"

Just because he didn't go to this school didn't mean he couldn't get suspended from it. Getting kicked out of school was getting kicked out of school. That's all he wanted.

"Pick those up!" his mother ordered.

"I hate it! I hate it!" he shouted, jumping up and down, scattering the coupons, kicking them back up into the air. He slammed his palm down on the counter. "I hate it here!"

He had to work quickly, invent a crisis that would get him thrown out of the building before his mother got a chance to see the principal.

"Jacob, I said pick those up!"

"Young man!"

He kicked the rack holding the time cards of the teachers. The cards flew into the air.

"Young man!"

"Jacob!" His mother grabbed his shoulder and squeezed. He stopped jumping. His mother's grip could turn bricks into sand. It radiated pain to all parts of his body. It turned his thoughts into static electricity.

The secretary disappeared into the principal's office.

"What has gotten into you?" his mother asked.

"Come right in," the secretary said, reappearing.

His mother relaxed her grip. Jacob lunged for the exit. His mother caught his wrist and pulled him back. Though he tried to hook his foot around every piece of furniture they passed, Jacob found himself standing straight and tall in front of Mrs. Kaufman's desk, with Mrs. Kaufman, a short, grey-haired woman, standing on the other side.

His mother gripped his shoulder again. Barbs of pain shot up and down his right side, curling his toes and bringing tears to his eyes.

"Please sit down," Mrs. Kaufman said, sounding severe but confused. She stared at Jacob like he was a suspect in a police lineup.

His mother slid her grip down his arm to his wrist as they both sat down in big overstuffed chairs. Her grip was still so secure that if he tried to escape, he would have to leave his right arm behind. As if to prevent that possibility, Mrs. Kaufman walked over to the door and closed it before sitting down.

"I think we can both agree that Jacob has very special needs," his mother said. It was the first line of her rehearsed monologue.

"I don't understand," Mrs. Kaufman said.

"No. I agree. He should be punished. What he did was very wrong."

"What did you do?" Mrs. Kaufman asked, leaning forward.

He couldn't answer her. He couldn't speak. His mother was about to give a carefully thought-out speech to the wrong audience. She was about to argue his case in front of the wrong judge in the wrong court. His prank had worked. Now what?

"I asked you," Mrs. Kaufman said sternly. "What did you do?"

Should he confess? He couldn't. He would make his mother look like a fool. How could he do this to her?

"I'm not asking you to dismiss his behavior yesterday," his mother said. "I've spoken to him about it. But I think you could understand it better if you understood what causes it."

"What did you do?" Mrs. Kaufman asked, showing her rising frustration. "Please tell me. What did you do?"

What could he do? There was no turning back. The only safe way to leave was by force. Violence. A reasonable discussion would be too damaging. He had to save his mother. He had to get himself kicked out now, suspended from a school he had never been in before.

"He hit me first," Jacob whined. "You didn't see that, did you? No. No. No. You didn't even care. No. All you did was walk in and blame me."

Mrs. Kaufman looked at him suspiciously. He returned her gaze with the most sullen look he could muster. He would imitate Shawn Scott, a kid from his old school. Shawn was sneaky and irritating, always the first to deny doing anything wrong. If there was a fight in the back of the class, if there was a window broken or a pencil missing, Shawn would always whine, "I didn't do it! It wasn't my fault. All you ever do is blame me."

"Jacob's not a bad kid," his mother said.

"Just because I threw the desk at him!" he whined in Shawn's nasal voice. "Just because I threw the desk at him, you yell at me. Like he didn't do anything—like he didn't do nothing."

"What desk?" his mother asked.

"Who?" Mrs. Kaufman asked. "Who did you throw a desk at?"

"No. No. No. All you cared about was that dumb desk. Jeeesh!" Jacob cursed. Did he sound authentic?

"What desk, Jacob?" his mother asked. "You never mentioned anything about a desk."

"In what class was this?" Mrs. Kaufman asked.

"No. No. All you did was blame me. You didn't even see what he did. No. Just because I threw the ant farm and hit him with the window pole. No. You didn't even care what he did first."

"Jacob," his mother asked. "What are you talking about?"

"What ant farm? What window pole?" Mrs. Kaufman asked.

61

"No. No. Just because the window broke. Like it was my fault. Like he didn't make me do it. Like everything is my fault. Like when the stink bomb went off and . . ."

Mrs. Kaufman was smiling. She was leaning across the desk, holding his arm and smiling.

"Now, stop it," she said, almost laughing. "Now, c'mon, stop it. Who sent you guys down here? Marty?"

"Who's Marty?" Jacob asked, utterly lost.

"Stop it. Tell me," Mrs. Kaufman said. She turned to Jacob's mother, who seemed bewildered. "Marty sent you guys, right? This kid doesn't go to this school. I never saw this kid before. What is this? The joke Marty plays on all the new principals? Very funny."

"Who's Marty?" Jacob asked.

"Jacob," his mother said. "What's going on?"

"Tell me," Mrs. Kaufman began again. "Tell me Marty's not the craziest district superintendent you've ever heard of. What does he think? Just because I'm a new principal, I don't know who goes here or what's happening in the building?"

"What school is this?" his mother asked.

"P.S. 103," Mrs. Kaufman answered.

"Jacob," his mother said, squeezing his arm. "You don't go to P.S. 103."

9

They left the building and headed directly to a pay phone. His mother called his father in Chicago. His father arrived at LaGuardia Airport four hours later. By two thirty Jacob and his father were strolling through the Hall of the Northwestern Pacific Indians in the Museum of Natural History.

It seemed the right place to be. Since Jacob could remember, his father had taken him to the museum once a week to help him forget his asthma and escape the nastiness of city life. Standing in front of the museum's stuffed birds, its glass-encased bears and beavers, and its painted-forest landscapes was the closest Jacob had ever come to nature. The allergies that went with his asthma prevented him from visiting a zoo or taking a walk in the woods. Making up stories about everything they saw, from the dinosaurs to the meteors, his father made Jacob feel as if the museum belonged to the two of them.

Jacob had thought of taking Cynthia there. But that was before the disaster in the principal's office, before that lost look on his mother's face. Now his father was here but everything was falling apart.

"See that sort of owlish face on the top of that totem

pole?" his father asked, pointing to the top of a wildly carved, twenty-foot pole.

"Yes," Jacob said, anticipating a story.

"I carved that," his father said, looking quite serious.

"You did a great job," Jacob said, going along with the routine.

"I did. It's been fooling the crowds for the last thirty years. They all think some Haida tribesman carved it. They don't know I did it when I was thirteen. Climbed to the top of the pole when the guard was napping. Used my Swiss Army knife."

"You did a great job. It looks real," Jacob said, smiling. He had not been to the museum in nearly a year, since his father had begun his tour with *A Chorus Line*. "Dad, I don't want to go back to school."

"So I hear," his father said, walking along slowly to a glass cabinet of arrowheads and spear points. As usual his father looked messy. He wasn't shaven. His dark hair was uncombed. His left shirt collar was sticking up out of his sweater. Only a costume director could get his father to look neat.

"You have to go back to Chicago?" Jacob asked.

"Yes," his father said, putting his hand on Jacob's back and leading him through the dark hall.

"How come?" Jacob asked, turning around and looking up at his father. "Why can't you stay? Why can't you act in New York?"

"I'm doing what I can." His father spoke softly. He looked hurt.

Jacob began to cry. He found a bench in a dark corner and sat down. His father sat next to him, put his arm around Jacob, and hugged him.

64

"You came back to tell me you're putting me in that Special 10 class," Jacob said, looking down at the floor. "I'm not going."

"What class do you want to be in?" his father asked, rubbing Jacob's back.

"Not in that class. Mr. Macombo said they put on a play about themselves. Their teacher makes everybody in the school feel sorry for them. I'm not putting on any play."

"What do you want, Jacob?" his father asked.

"I just want to be a regular kid! Why can't I just be a regular kid? Why do I have to have asthma? Why do I have to be so weak?"

"Jacob, you're not weak," his father said. "Anybody who has passed the tests your asthma has put you through is not weak."

"Everybody treats me like I'm a weakling."

"You're not. Every time your asthma has challenged you, you have knocked it flat on its backside and walked away."

"You make me sound like Isaac."

"There's something inside of you that's stronger than Isaac," his father said. "You know that."

"Then why does everybody worry about me?"

"Well, you're just going to have to stand up and show them they don't need to," his father said, looking at his watch.

"Why are you looking at your watch?" Jacob asked.

"Jacob, I've seen you play hockey with kids twice your size," his father said, rising. "I've seen you go flying towards the net on a breakaway, and I don't understand why—"

"Where are you going?"

"I have a show this evening, son," his father said softly. "I have to be back in Chicago."

"Why can't you stay in New York? Why are you always leaving?"

"Jacob, I'm an actor. I'm . . ."

"You're my father! Why do you have to go back? Why?"

His father leaned over and kissed Jacob on the top of his head. "Jacob," he said quietly but firmly. "I love you. And we're doing the best for you. This class is flexible and will be able to help you out if you miss too much school. It's got two teachers and eleven students. You have to be bright, very bright, to get into it. We're putting you in the Special 10 class. There'll be kids there in the same situation you're in. And you won't have to be in the play."

"I'm not going into that class."

"Jacob, just go in there with your hockey jersey on."

"No."

"Jacob, I have to get back to Mom," his father said, looking sad and tired. "I have a show tonight. I have a three-day weekend next month. Maybe we could go away to Cooperstown, to the Baseball Hall of Fame. Just the two of us."

"No."

"I have to get back, son."

Slowly Jacob followed his father out of the dark museum into the afternoon light. Across the street the trees of Central Park shook their red and gold leaves in a gentle wind.

Reaching their building, Jacob refused to go upstairs with his father.

"Tell Mom I'll be up at six," he said.

His father leaned over to hug him and kiss him good-bye. Jacob backed away.

"Jacob."

"Bye." He turned and began to run. He ran up the block to the blind man's newsstand.

"I'm back, it's after three, the police aren't going to come for me, you're not going to lose your license, I'm not going anywhere, and I know your name is Theodore," Jacob said in one breath. "I know that's your name because I heard a man call you that."

"Dillinger?" Theodore asked, leaning out of the window of the booth.

"I'll be your friend. I'll work for you. I belong here," Jacob responded adamantly.

A tall man in a blue suit approached the stand and picked a magazine off the racks. "*Forbes*," the man said, and placed a bill on the ledge of Theodore's window.

"What are you giving me here?" Theodore asked the man.

"A five," the man said.

"He's telling the truth," Jacob said, standing on his tiptoes to see the bill.

The man glanced down at Jacob with annoyance.

"Dillinger, what are you doing there? You sound like you're out of breath," said Theodore.

"Sometimes when I run, I start to wheeze. It's from my asthma. It's nothing," he said, and took his spray. Leaning against the booth beside Theodore's window he held his breath, then slowly exhaled. His lungs cleared. "Don't worry," he reassured Theodore. "If anybody steals a paper, I'll be able to run after them. I might just have to take my medicine after the police come to arrest him. Now, what do you want me to do?"

"First of all," Theodore said, "don't run after anybody.

You see somebody steal a paper, you just go up to that cop on 90th Street and point out the thief to him. He'll take care of the running. You see that cop?"

"Yes."

"Good. You let him take care of the chasing and arresting. His name is Jon. Officer Rinde. He knows me. You just walk over to him and tell him who stole what. If he shoots the guy, I'll let you keep the bullets."

"But what if I'm right here, and I see somebody trying to steal some gum or a newspaper? You don't want me to make a citizen's arrest? I know how to read somebody their rights. Listen. 'You have the right to—' "

"No. You just walk up to Jon. If you see somebody who you think might be about to steal something, you just start up a conversation with them. They won't steal while you're talking to them. You got that?"

"Yes."

"Good. Now pick up *The New York Times* and read to me some interesting news. Nobody's read to me from *The New York Times* in years. I used to have a college kid come over and do that, but that was years ago. You can read, right, Dillinger?"

"Of course I can read," Jacob said.

"Good. After we're done with the news, you'll read me some stories from some of those magazines. I used to love to listen to stories from *The New Yorker*. And, Dillinger?"

"Yes?"

"If the policeman catches you looking at any of the sexy magazines on the rack, he might arrest you. Your mother would have to go to the precinct to bail you out. So don't look at any of the sexy magazines."

Jacob laughed, then looked up at the rack holding the

68

sexy magazines. He gasped. He looked down at his sneakers. Cautiously he moved his gaze away from the ground to the stack of *New York Times* beneath Theodore's window. He removed the second copy from the stack and read aloud the first headline that caught his eye.

" 'Missile Treaty up for Vote,' You want to hear that?"

"Fine. Sounds fine."

Jacob began to read. He spoke in a loud, clear voice, so that Theodore could hear him above the noises of the street. He read the article dramatically, as if he were Lincoln reading the Gettysburg Address. Theodore, however, interrupted him repeatedly to explain the meaning and significance of what he was reading. While Jacob pretended to be frustrated by these interruptions, he secretly appreciated them. Without them he would not have understood most of the article.

After he finished reading about missiles, he read a few more articles scattered throughout the paper. With Theodore's explanations and opinions, Jacob's understanding and interest in what he was reading increased.

Cars honked their horns. Trucks backfired. Every few minutes an ambulance or a police car got stuck in the traffic on Broadway, and its siren would wail desperately. When this happened, people walked by with their heads bowed and their fingers in their ears, and Jacob and Theodore waited. Jacob wondered how Theodore could spend day after day in the noise and the dirt. He wondered what it would be like to take him to the Museum of Natural History and tell him stories about all of the posed animals behind their glass windows.

When the sirens passed, they resumed, Jacob reading and Theodore teaching. They paused for customers, for teenagers bopping by with their violently booming radios, and for drunks who stopped to rant and curse at their invisible enemies.

At these breaks Jacob leaned against the racks of the booth and surveyed the street as if he were an aristocrat reviewing his estate. It felt luxurious to be standing in a place he owned while everyone else was forced to move on. And when a customer came to the booth, his booth, and asked for a magazine or candy, Jacob felt as if he were in the center of the city.

After they finished an article on city corruption, Theodore asked Jacob to read aloud a story from *The New Yorker*. Jacob picked up the magazine and began to read a tale about a poor man in India whose only possessions were two goats. Just as Jacob reached the part where the man was about to receive a fortune for those goats, Theodore stopped him.

"That's fine, Dillinger. You can finish tomorrow."

"I can stay. I can read more," Jacob offered.

"I'll see you tomorrow. After three. You'd better get home and do your homework."

"But I don't have any homework," Jacob insisted.

"Home, Dillinger. Remember what page we're up to."

Jacob returned the magazine to the rack. He put his hand on top of Theodore's right hand. It was rough and scratchy, yet warm.

"I'll be back tomorrow," Jacob said, and slowly but cheerfully began to walk home.

still have nice eyes?"

Jacob looked up the stairs leading to his building. Cynthia was sitting on the top step. She was wearing a long black dress and a boy's button-down grey shirt. She had some records on her lap.

"So I still have nice eyes?" she asked again.

"Yes," Jacob said, and immediately ran out of anything else to say.

"Thanks," she smiled. "I didn't get suspended," she apologized. "Mr. Macombo told me he considers his school a family. He said, 'I don't enjoy punishing members of my school family. Do you understand, Cynthia?' I said, 'Yes, I understand. If Mrs. Pelham is a part of my family, that should be punishment enough.' "

Jacob laughed. "Did you get into trouble?"

"That was the whole idea," Cynthia said, laughing. "But it didn't work. I don't think they know what to do with me anymore. I think they might even stick me in Ms. Brace's class, 'cause I know how to read. That's where you started off, right?"

"Yes," Jacob said.

"So maybe you could go back. We could be classmates."

He couldn't answer her. He wasn't going back to school.

"So anyway, right after school I ran home and changed. Then I ran over here. I got your address from your card in the office the day I called you. So, hi."

"Hi." His heart was racing.

"I brought some music," she said, standing, holding out a record to Jacob.

Jacob climbed up a step and reached for the album. "*The Best of Irving Berlin*?" he read aloud.

"That's Fred Astaire," Cynthia said, pointing at the photograph of the man on the cover. He was wearing a top hat and tails. There was a cane tucked under his arm. His hands were in his pockets. His black shoes were pointed. He seemed to be dancing in thin air.

"It's old. It's old-fashioned," she said. "You want to go upstairs and hear it? I can show you how to dance to it. I know all of those old dances. I can teach you how. I've watched all of those old movies. I've memorized each step. I'm really good. I can show you how to be like Fred Astaire. You can be my partner."

"My mother's upstairs," Jacob said.

"That's okay. She won't mind. It's old-fashioned stuff. It's . . . it's romantic. Look. I'm dressed nice."

"You look pretty," Jacob admitted.

"So let's go."

"I can't."

"I can show you."

"I can't dance."

"But I'll teach you. You could get black pants, and you could wear your grey shirt. We could be partners. We could be special. We could practice every day after school."

"I work after school," Jacob said, thinking of Theodore.

"We could practice before school."

"Where?"

"In Central Park! I have the record on tape. I could bring my tape player. You could meet me tomorrow morning at seven at the 89th Street entrance to the Park."

"I can't. I'm allergic."

"Nobody's allergic to this dancing. It's in black and white. It's like being in a movie."

"No. I'm allergic to the Park."

"You won't be. We'll be dancing."

"I want to, but . . ."

"C'mon, Jacob. I need a partner. And you're perfect. You already have a grey shirt. And you have big hands. And you said I have pretty eyes. C'mon. I can't dance by myself. I need you."

He pictured her alone in the park. He pictured her sitting beside him on the steps in the school. She smiled at him.

"All right," he said.

"Good! Good. Because you know, we have to start young if we're going to be good."

"I have to go upstairs now," Jacob said, returning the album. He pointed up to his window. "She's probably already started to panic."

"Good-bye, then . . . Jacob," Cynthia said, shaking his hand.

"Good-bye, Cynthia."

Watching her race up the block, moving more like a wide receiver than a ballerina, Jacob felt a strange combination of fear and intense joy. His whole body was humming; his whole world was humming.

He had a friend. She had pretty eyes. He liked her. She had changed her clothes for him. She made him laugh. He

73

had found somebody who didn't worry about him, who knew there was nothing wrong with him. Maybe he was in love.

But he couldn't meet her in the park. It didn't matter what type of dancing they did. The park was blanketed with fallen leaves. Mold grew on those leaves, and mold spores filled the air. He was terribly allergic to mold spores. What could he do? If he didn't go, she would be hurt. If he did go, he could become ill, seriously ill, right in front of her. Some dance partner. He wouldn't be able to stand.

No. He *would* meet her in the park tomorrow. God would protect him. He loved her.

When he got upstairs, his mother asked him where he had been.

"Out" was all he said.

"I spoke to your principal," she said. "Your *real* principal. I'm going to see him tomorrow. There's something going on with the Special 10 classes in your district, and there's going to be a meeting. He wants me to come. You'll stay with Isaac. You'll go to school with him for the day."

"Fine," Jacob said, picking up his mother's copy of the *Times*. He opened up the first section to the editorial page and plopped down on the couch.

He would meet Cynthia, then rush back to his apartment in time to leave with Isaac. Let his mother talk to his principal, Jacob thought. He wasn't going back to that school. He had Cynthia. He didn't need school to be with her. School would just make them different people. He had Theodore and the newsstand. That was enough.

He found an essay about civil liberties and began to read it closely. He thought of the questions he would ask Theodore, and wrote them down in the margins. The rest of the evening slipped by, and it wasn't until he turned off his lights at eleven that he realized that in eight hours he would be with Cynthia. He looked up at the slats supporting Isaac's bunk and thought of the little stick-on stars that were glimmering above. He thought of Cynthia in the park and found himself imagining the two of them in that wheat field in Kansas at night. They were dancing.

III

"Don't tell Mom," Isaac said from his top bunk, "but I passed the first audition."

"What?" Jacob asked. He had almost forgotten he had an older brother.

"I said, don't tell Mom, but I passed the first audition. I auditioned for the school's first production. I got called back. I have a reading tomorrow."

"Why shouldn't I tell Mom?" Jacob asked.

"Because I don't want her to get her hopes up."

"Why should she get her hopes up? She doesn't even want you to be an actor. She says she doesn't want either of us to get into acting. She wants us both to become lawyers or doctors. She wants us to become normal people and have money."

"No, she's just saying that to make sure you do well in school. I think she really wants me to be an actor."

"What do you mean to make sure *I* do well in school?"

"Well, you know. We're all worried about you."

"What? What do you mean, 'we'? Don't you be worried about me, Isaac. And what makes you so sure you'll get the part? Dad couldn't even get a part in New York."

"Jacob, this isn't Broadway. It's J.H.S. 78."

"So. It's still New York. You think you're better than Dad? You think you're just going to get the part because you want it? You just think everything's so easy. Like you deserve it."

"You're not happy for me?"

"Break a leg," Jacob mumbled.

"Thanks. I hope you bring me good luck."

"How am I going to bring you good luck?" Jacob asked.

"You're coming to school with me, tomorrow. Didn't Mom tell you?"

"Oh, that's right. I forgot I was going to be your prisoner. What time is the audition?"

"Seven-thirty. We'll have to leave a little before seven. I hope that's not too early for you."

"It's not too early," Jacob said, knowing that Isaac would miss his audition anyway. Jacob was not going to disappoint Cynthia to be with his brother, especially for something that had to do with the theater.

"I'll set my alarm for six," Isaac said. "I'm sorry. I know it's a little early. But then again, you'll probably get to see some fine acting. It might be worth it."

"I'm sure it will. I can't wait," Jacob said. "So don't be sorry. Just go to sleep. Now."

"You're right. I'm going to need my sleep."

"You'll get it," Jacob assured him, his plan already formulated.

He would create an "accident." As soon as he was sure Isaac was asleep, he would climb up to his bunk and move Isaac's clock back by three hours. When Isaac's alarm sounded, though it would read six, it would really be nine.

He would set his own clock for six, time enough to get dressed and get down to the park to meet Cynthia. He would return in time to get undressed and fall asleep until nine, when Isaac's clock sounded. Then he would rush off to school with Isaac for the audition, for which they would be three hours late.

"Good night, little brother," Isaac said. "Wake me if you need anything."

"Good night, Isaac." Jacob said.

"Good night, Jacob. And thanks for the stars."

Isaac turned off his light.

Suddenly Jacob felt sorry for his brother. Where did that come from? It was an entirely new feeling. It made Jacob angry with himself. He tried to shake it, but couldn't. It didn't seem fair. How come Isaac was allowed to prevent him from seeing Cynthia, but he wasn't allowed to prevent Isaac from going to some stupid audition without feeling bad?

He hated the theater. Though his teachers had told him he was a good actor, he wasn't—he was a good liar and storyteller. He had always refused to be in the class play. The theater was like his asthma. It ruled his life. It took his father away from him. It made his mother crazy. It made his family poor.

Now the theater was trying to keep him from Cynthia. He hated that. After what seemed like hours, Jacob quietly got out of bed and climbed the ladder up to Isaac's bunk. He tickled Isaac's left foot. Isaac jerked his foot away, but didn't wake. Satisfied, Jacob crawled onto and along Isaac's bed to his alarm clock. He turned Isaac's clock three hours back and crawled into the bottom bunk.

Jacob lay on his bed with his hands tucked under his head and tried to calm himself, shut down his imagination, which kept him too charged up with images of Cynthia in the park. He saw her smile. He saw her offer her hand.

He turned over on his stomach and pushed his face into his pillow. He wanted to smother his thoughts, blacken his imagination. He wanted to rush sleep, rush the night. He wanted to see her dressed in black and grey. He wanted to be her partner. Gradually his wishes slipped into dreams and Jacob fell asleep.

A nightmare woke him. He bolted upright to escape it. An ugly fear, a sensation of having nearly drowned, made him grip his blankets and anxiously wait for his sleepiness to clear. Slowly, as he peered through the darkness of his room, he began to recognize the outlines of familiar objects, of his desk, his hockey stick, his globe. He became calm. He remembered his dream.

He had been with Theodore, who had given him a pair of dark glasses to wear. He had put them on and become blind. Theodore had asked for them back, but Jacob couldn't remove them. Somehow Cynthia was there, but he couldn't see her. She had asked him to come with her, but he could only reach out for her in the dark.

Cynthia! What time was it? He picked up his alarm clock. Three A.M. Wait. That wasn't the real time, he remembered. He had changed it. Wait. How had he changed it? He had moved it back three hours. That was it. Why? Something to do with Isaac's audition. Something to do with sneaking out to see Cynthia. Three hours back. Then what time was it? Three hours forward. It was three . . . it was six A.M. He had to get up.

He shuffled into the kitchen to fix himself breakfast. He poured Cheerios into a bowl and sliced up a peach. Each slice dropping into the bowl plonked loudly and sounded unruly in the dark, quiet apartment. He poured some apple juice into the bowl. As usual, he wondered what cereal tasted like with milk. He couldn't have any dairy products. "When you were a baby," his mother had told him, "I couldn't breast-feed you. You were allergic."

That was his problem, he told himself. It wasn't his asthma. He was allergic to his mother.

He was falling asleep. He abandoned his cereal half-eaten, slowly rose, and shuffled into the bathroom, where he brushed his teeth and splashed cold water onto his face. He found a bottle of his father's after-shave in the medicine cabinet. He sprinkled a few drops onto his hands, then slapped his cheeks. He began sneezing wildly. He was allergic to the scent. Again he splashed cold water onto his face, this time to wash away the irritating fragrance.

He needed to dress. He needed a grey shirt and black pants. His grey shirt was somewhere in the hamper. He would have to wear a white shirt instead. Furtively he rummaged through his and Isaac's drawers until he found the white shirt he had worn a year ago to his cousin Noah's bar mitzvah. He popped two chest buttons putting the shirt on. He had grown and put on some weight in the past year. Maybe his parents were right when they said he was getting healthier. The cuffs came to about two inches above his wrist. No problem. He would roll up his sleeves. He felt it made him look more masculine anyway. It showed off his forearms, which he thought were muscular from once having worked out with weights.

He put on the pants that went with the shirt and noticed that the cuffs exposed quite a section of his legs above his ankles. No problem. He could fill the space with black socks and his new black high-tops.

Before leaving, he looked out of the window. It was dark.

Too dark. That meant rain. Then what? Would she still be there? Maybe she would show, just to bring him back to her place. They could dance in the lobby of her building, softly, with the music a whisper. Afterwards, he would convince her to cut school. He would take her to a movie. In black and white, he guessed.

He grabbed his umbrella and left.

He stepped out of his building onto the street and immediately found himself very much alone. Where was everybody? The block was so empty. A crumpled paper bag tumbled by his legs. From somewhere uptown a police-car siren wailed. He looked at the buildings that rose up on either side of him. Their windows were dark and lifeless. He began to feel anxious, vulnerable. He walked quietly down the block towards Amsterdam Avenue, pursued by the sound of his own footsteps. He gripped his umbrella as if it were a saber.

The grey steel gates were pulled down in front of all of the stores along Amsterdam Avenue. The streetlights changed from green to red, and the sign across the street flashed DON'T WALK. Though there wasn't a car in sight, Jacob waited. Emptied of all of its people, the city seemed alive and very aware of him.

But where was everybody? Shouldn't somebody be out, delivering papers or fish or fruit? Where were they? The sign across the street flashed WALK. Jacob obeyed.

He reached the entrance on 89th Street. It was on a hill overlooking a sandy playing field. At the edge of the field drifted a thin grey mist that spread slowly, turning black as it receded into the park.

Where was Cynthia?

She had fled with the others. Jacob kicked the ground.

81

He shook his fists at the sky. He cursed and began to cry. He was on the corner of 89th Street and Central Park West, roughly the center of the island of Manhattan, and he was alone. He had been abandoned by seven million people. He kicked the column of an old-fashioned cast-iron clock. The metal column rang like a bell. Jacob looked up. The clock read four A.M. Somehow seven million people had snuck out of the city in less than five hours. How did they do that without waking him? They must have been very sneaky.

Wait. It was four A.M. No. Yes, it was four A.M. What was he doing out at this hour?

He turned around and began to walk briskly towards home.

12

urry, wake up. We almost overslept," Isaac said, shaking Jacob's shoulder. "Hey, wake up. We're lucky your alarm went off. My clock must be broken. It's three hours slow. C'mon. Get up."

Something was buzzing inside Jacob's head. "Leave me alone. I'm tired," he said, pushing Isaac away. "I want to go back to sleep. I don't have school today."

Isaac was laughing.

Jacob reached for his alarm clock and turned off the buzzing.

Isaac was laughing so hard, he had to sit down. Jacob squinted at his brother, who was wearing his blue Rangers jersey.

"Isaac, stop it. Why are you laughing?"

"Jacob, why are you so dressed up? You going to a bar mitzvah? Since when did you start sleeping with your dress clothes on? You couldn't find your pajamas?"

Jacob quickly kicked the blankets off his legs. He stared in disbelief at his feet.

"I like the black high-tops, Jacob," Isaac said, still laughing. "All you need is your yarmulke and your basketball. Why are you dressed like that?"

"Isaac, what time is it?"

"Seven. We'd be late except you're already dressed. Unless . . . unless you want to put on a tie, too."

It was seven. Cynthia, if she showed, was waiting for him at the park. He could never get there in time. She wouldn't wait. She would remember his making excuses. She would suspect that he had been teasing her when he said yes. She was standing alone in Central Park. She was wearing black and grey, and she had her tape player and her Irving Berlin tapes, and he was not coming.

"Isaac, everything bad that has ever happened to me has been your fault."

"Let me get dressed," Isaac said, standing up, looking at Jacob curiously. He removed his jersey. He was growing hair on his chest. Jacob was angry. It was as if Isaac was purposefully becoming an adult in order to sneak up and take the place of their father. "I'll buy us donuts on the way to school," Isaac said. "We can eat them in the auditorium while we wait."

"I don't understand, Isaac. It's like it was all meant to be this way. There was no choice about who was going to be happy and who was going to have everything bad happen to him. And you were picked to be the happy one."

"I'm not always happy, Jacob," Isaac said, putting on his jeans. "And bad things don't only happen to you."

"No. Nothing bad can happen to you, Isaac. I know it. I do. I've tried to do stuff to you, to play practical jokes on you, to get you scared or to get some guy to fight you. But it's never worked. Every time I've tried something, something bad happened to me instead. I set your clock back. I wanted you to miss your audition."

"I can understand that, Jacob. You don't want me to be

an actor, like Dad. But I don't think you have to worry. I'll never leave you and Mom. I'd miss you too much. And I'd worry about you."

Isaac put on his shirt. "I understand, Jacob," he said, looking at himself in the mirror. "You think this shirt is too boring?"

It was a plain blue shirt.

"Isaac, don't say you understand. Don't. From now on, you can't understand me anymore. You're not allowed."

Isaac picked up his script. "C'mon, we'd better get going," he said, pushing up the sleeves of his jacket.

"And why are you wearing *that* jacket?" Jacob demanded. It's too big on you. It doesn't fit. It'll never fit you."

"It brings me good luck," Isaac said, shrugging his shoulders.

Jacob grabbed him by the sleeve. "Isaac, I wanted something bad to happen to you. And today, I . . . Everything's gone wrong. And it's your fault. And I don't want to be with you. And I don't want you to be happy. And I'm going to—I'm going to do something today that's going to mess things up for you."

Isaac looked down at Jacob, then back to his script. He flipped through the pages.

"I understand," he said, closing the script. He smiled weakly at Jacob, then looked down at his own hands. They were trembling slightly. "Wow. I guess I really am nervous about the audition. I didn't think I was."

"You'll do fine," Jacob mumbled, looking away from Isaac's hands.

It was a dark and cloudy Wednesday morning. Neither of them spoke as they walked down Amsterdam Avenue to Isaac's school. The heavy city air, carrying the exhaust fumes from the slow-moving buses and trucks, irritated Jacob's throat and made his eyes water. It made it difficult for him to concentrate on what he would need to do to ruin Isaac's audition. He thought instead of ways he could track down Cynthia, apologize, explain, get another chance. He could wait for her after school. No, he had to be with Theodore then. He could sneak in to see her during lunch, walk by the yard during recess. He would find a way.

When they finally arrived at Isaac's school, Jacob reached for the auditorium door. Isaac stopped him before he could open it.

"Wait," Isaac said, his voice cracking. "I just wanted to tell you something."

"What?"

But Isaac couldn't answer him. He couldn't speak. He looked pale. There were tears in his eyes. He bit his bottom lip to stop it from quivering.

Jacob suddenly felt ashamed. He was responsible for this. His brother appeared on the verge of a nervous breakdown. One more prank and Jacob would be visiting him in one of those institutions where everybody wears their pajamas in the daytime and makes pictures out of beans and shells.

Isaac wiped his tears on his jacket sleeve. Again he started to say something but stopped himself. He looked as if he was about to cry.

Suddenly Jacob saw himself as a cruel person. It was all clear and ugly. He had been abusive to Isaac since he could remember. For years he had been trying to punish Isaac

86

for stealing his health, his chance for happiness. He felt as if he and Isaac had been placed on opposite ends of a seesaw, and he was joylessly stuck on the ground, weighted down by his asthma, while Isaac floated up on the other end, weightless. For years, he now realized, he had been trying to raise himself up by bringing Isaac down.

Now that Isaac was about to tumble to the ground, Jacob felt guilty. Isaac was not responsible for his problems. He was. Why make Isaac suffer along with him?

"Don't worry," Jacob said, reaching up and grabbing Isaac's shoulder. "I won't sabotage your audition."

Isaac looked puzzled.

"I won't pick on you anymore," Jacob reassured him.

"You don't pick on me," Isaac said.

"Yes I do," Jacob admitted.

"No you don't."

"Yes I do," Jacob insisted.

"No you don't," Isaac also insisted.

"Yes I do," Jacob said. "I put crumbs in your bed. I blame you for things that I do. I tell kids to beat you up. I play practical jokes on you, and I play with all of your crazy fears."

"Oh," Isaac said after some thought. "That stuff doesn't bother me."

"What do you mean, it doesn't bother you? Yes it does."

"No it doesn't," Isaac said.

"Yes it does, Isaac. I torment you."

"No you don't."

"Yes I do. Mom even says I do. I torment you."

"You torment me?" Isaac asked.

"You never noticed?"

87

"No."

Something had flip-flopped. He couldn't get Isaac to admit that he had even been a pest.

Isaac wasn't being heroic. He was being honest. He really didn't feel tormented. Jacob had never so much as irritated him. It was all hopeless. "I haven't even made your life a little difficult?"

"Nope."

"Then what are you so upset about?"

"I just wanted to tell you, Jacob, that if Mom and Dad were ever killed, like in a plane crash, I would take care of you. I would. I just wanted you to know that. I didn't want you to worry."

"Why would Mom and Dad be killed in a plane crash?"

"You never know, Jacob."

"What are you planning to do to Mom and Dad?" Jacob asked.

He stood still. Isaac wasn't on the verge of a nervous breakdown. He was on the verge of killing their parents just to prove he was a good older brother.

Maybe he should go live with Theodore.

He kept the idea to himself, as if it were a stolen toy. He played with it secretly as he sat through Isaac's audition. His parents didn't really know him. He was just their son with asthma. Isaac was their son with no problems. Theodore understood him, didn't worry about him, knew he could take care of himself. He could start all over, living with Theodore.

Isaac soon pulled Jacob out of his reverie. He not only remembered his lines, but performed them as if he believed them. As John Adams in *1776*, Isaac's passion for the Revolution was stirring. Jacob found himself wanting to run back home, get on his horse, and ride down to Philadelphia to sign the Declaration. He was convinced. America must rule itself!

Apparently Isaac also convinced the director, who asked him to wait around until the auditions were over. He got the part.

After several hours of classes, Isaac finally had to go to rehearsals. Jacob said good-bye and left the building. The early-morning clouds had cleared, and a cool breeze that smelled of autumn and the new year teased his memory. He thought of the first day of school a few years ago, when he was forced to sit down in the middle of a close football game because of his asthma. While he took his spray, a kid called him Pussy Katz, and other kids started chanting it. After attacking the first kid he could grab and getting beaten up, he ran from the school to the theater where his mother was rehearsing a play. He marched right up onto the stage, sat down on the couch next to his mother, and announced, in the middle of a scene, that he wanted her to change his name. After the director returned with ice for his puffy eye and paper towels for his bloody nose, his mother took him backstage.

"Jacob, in the plays we perform, your father and I take on new names all the time," she had said. "But it's just make-believe. We always have to come back to our real names and take care of our real problems."

She was wrong, Jacob thought, approaching Theodore's newsstand. Theodore had changed his name to Dillinger and his problems had disappeared. With Theodore he was proud of himself. He was a new kid. He wasn't running away from anything anymore. There was no more school. No more Ms. Brace, or Mr. Macombo, or Special 10 class.

"Hey, Theodore, it's Dillinger. I'm back," Jacob announced, stepping beside a tall man in a blue suit.

"Good," Theodore smiled. He tilted his head towards Jacob, but appeared to be looking just past him. "Lenny," Theodore said to the tall man, "meet Dillinger, my new buddy and co-worker."

"Pleased to meet you, Dillinger," Lenny said, offering his hand.

"Hi," Jacob said, and proudly took the man's hand.

"That boy there's decided to leave the world of crime for the world of journalism and literature," Theodore said.

"Good choice," Lenny said.

"I read to him. I'm a good reader," Jacob boasted.

"So I've heard," Lenny said. "Sounds like Theodore's pretty lucky to have you around."

He could live with Theodore, Jacob thought. They could be roommates. Theodore needed him. And neither of them felt sorry for the other. He could start his whole life over again.

Lenny said good-bye and left.

"All right, Dillinger, let's begin with page one of *The New York Times*. Before it rains. It smells like it's going to start coming down any minute."

Jacob began to read an article about a skirmish in the Middle East. His thoughts, however, drifted away from the article. Sadly, he realized he hadn't found a new home. He had just found another place to hide. Home and school, his asthma, those kids—they were waiting for him. They would catch him again. He thought of Cynthia.

"It's not a religious war," Theodore said, interrupting his thoughts.

"I knew that," Jacob replied automatically.

"No you didn't," Theodore laughed, and explained the history of the conflict. Theodore knew everything.

It began to pour. Jacob pressed his back against the booth and stood beside its tiny window. Above him the rain hit the overhanging tin roof, sounding like a low roll on a snare drum. Jacob put aside his newspaper and noticed how Theodore seemed lost in delight, listening to the rain.

"Hello, sky," Theodore smiled.

Jacob turned to watch the people on the street scramble for cover. They panicked. Some ducked into doorways, while too many crowded under a bus shelter. Some placed already-soggy newspapers over their heads. One man dumped his groceries out of a plastic bag into the garbage and stuck the bag on his head. Jacob began to describe what he saw, shouting above the rain, and Theodore laughed.

This is the way things can be, Jacob told himself. Then he told Theodore all about Cynthia.

"Don't give up on her, Dillinger," Theodore said. "You need a partner as much as she does."

13

"Did anybody call?" Jacob asked, sitting down for dinner.

"For you?" his mother asked.

"Yes," Jacob said.

"No."

"Nobody called, then hung up when you answered?" Jacob asked. Maybe Cynthia had given up on him. Maybe she hated him for lying to her, for standing her up.

"No," his mother said.

"A girl didn't call and accidentally get the wrong number?"

"No," his mother said, putting his dinner before him: skinless chicken (he was allergic to the skin), tired mashed potatoes (he was allergic to milk, butter, and margerine), and limp, watery string beans.

Where was Cynthia? Did she hate him now? Had he missed his only chance?

A Beethoven piano sonata, coming from a small tape player atop the refrigerator, played softly. His mother believed in classical music at dinner, especially piano music. Since Jacob could remember, he had thought the two belonged together. Even outside, when he heard Beethoven, he thought of boiled chicken.

He needed to see Cynthia. Why? She made him feel like somebody entirely new, he realized. No asthma, no problems in school, nobody worrying about him. It was almost as if he was a character, and she had a part for him in some dance or story or movie in her imagination. It was dizzying. It was like stepping out of the thick, stuffy air that always seemed to be pressing down on him. Cynthia had exciting plans for him, and though he didn't know what they were, they had to be better than anybody else's. And she made him laugh. She made him feel like the two of them could get away with anything.

His mother hummed with the music. She poured him a glass of pear nectar. Jacob wondered what a milk shake tasted like. When he grew up and out of his allergies—his doctors had said that *might* happen, and his parents had promised it would—he would have a milk shake at every meal, a different flavor each night. He would start on Sunday with vanilla and work his way through chocolate, cherry, strawberry, peach, butterscotch, and banana. He closed his eyes and took a spoonful of mashed potatoes, trying to imagine a taste for them. They tasted like clothing. So did his chicken. He tried to distinguish between the two. The mashed potatoes were easier to chew. He wanted pizza. He wanted to be able to eat pizzas and milk shakes.

"Before the meeting on the Special 10 classes," his mother said, "I was telling Mr. Macombo about your performance at P.S. 103. I was telling him how, for a while at least, you had created a completely new personality for yourself, a new character with a new life. I told him how you had that poor principal and me believing you."

"I did my best."

"Your best is quite good," his mother said, looking a little proud, a little bewildered. "You'd impress quite a few directors with that performance. When I told Mr. Macombo, he was intrigued. I told him how we were a family of actors. Mr. Macombo mentioned something about a play in that Special 10 class."

"I'm not going into that class."

"He said that maybe you'd become a great actor someday," she said, laughing. "I told him I hoped not. I told him I want you to be anything but a poor, brilliant actor. But I admitted it might just be in your blood. You might have no choice."

"I'm not going to be an actor."

"I don't blame you, Jacob," his mother said. "But you were pretty impressive there in that principal's office. You became somebody else."

"I wanted to be somebody else," Jacob said, thinking of how he had wanted to be Theodore's son, as if he could erase his asthma by erasing his family. Now all he wanted to be was Cynthia's dancing partner. "I still want to be somebody else," he said quietly to himself.

His mother sat down opposite him and began to slice a banana into a container of yogurt. Yogurt gave Jacob terrible headaches. His mother ate it almost every evening, unless his father was home. Then she ordered Chinese food, though she still made Jacob his boiled chicken.

Jacob looked up at his mother. Her eyes were dark brown. Her dark hair was loose and fell about her face. He thought of the time she had painted her face white to play a ghost in a Japanese play.

"Ma, I feel like I'm in a prison," he said. "I can't go

anywhere. I can't do anything. I can't eat anything. There are all of these rules for what I can breathe or touch or smell. Why? Why am I being punished? What did I do?"

"You haven't done anything wrong, Jacob. Nobody has. Your father and I used to blame ourselves for your attacks, for your allergies. But it's nobody's fault. You have your asthma because there are a bunch of chemicals in your body that react incorrectly to other chemicals that you inhale, swallow, or touch. None of these chemicals are angry with you. None of them think. If any of them could think, they wouldn't be so stupid as to go wild every time you drank milk or smelled a flower. Nobody's being punished. Actually, you're not even being punished at school."

"What do you mean?"

"Mr. Macombo seemed very understanding. He said his school was one big family, and as a family, it has a responsibility to take care of its special kids."

"I'm not special," Jacob said firmly.

"Yes you are, Jacob. You're creative, imaginative, and clever."

"That's not the special he was talking about. He means special like in 'special needs.' I don't have any special needs."

"He took me over to the class. It's on the first floor."

"The kindergartners and the first-graders are on the first floor!" Jacob yelled.

"Jacob, there are some days when some kids can't climb four flights of steps. But, Jacob, they have gym three days a week."

"With who? With what other class?" Jacob asked angrily.

"Just by themselves. They get the whole gym to themselves," his mother said. "So they're not forced to compete with the other kids."

"But I want to compete with the other kids! I'm just as good as they are."

"Of course you are, Jacob. That's why they assign a boy to you from Ms. Brace's class to be your buddy. So you're still part of the sixth grade. He'll help you catch up on your assignments when you're sick, and he'll help you make friends. You'll have lunch together."

"Lunch together? I'm not going to eat with any kid who's been assigned to be my friend, like I'm his charity. I'm not going. You're not putting me in that class. I'm not going back to that school, either. Put me in another school."

"Jacob, even if we put you in another school, we'd have to put you in their Special 10 class."

"Then I'm not going back to school. I'll learn all I need to learn from Theodore."

"Who is Theodore?"

"He runs the newsstand on Broadway. I'm his friend. We work together." Jacob pushed away his plate. "We read the papers and magazines. He teaches me. I don't need school."

"Working? I didn't give you permission, Jacob. . . ."

"Dillinger. Theodore calls me Dillinger."

His mother ran her fingers through her hair and sighed. "When did you start working for—"

"Theodore. His name is Theodore. . . . This food is boring," he said, trying to hurt her. "It's boring."

He rose from the table, walked into his bedroom, and slammed the door behind him. He slumped onto his bed and punched his mattress. He punched his pillow.

"Why?" he shouted.

Why was she putting him into a class where each kid would be known for what was wrong with him? He'd be the kid with the asthma. Another kid would be the kid with diabetes, or kidney disease. And they'd be the class with the sick kids. How could Cynthia ever talk to a kid from a class like that? Why was his mother doing this to him? She was going to take him away from Theodore. She was going to take him away from Cynthia. He hated his mother. He hated his father. He began to pound the pillow.

"Jacob," his mother said from the other side of the door. "I'm sorry your dinner is boring. Maybe I can work on making dinners a little more interesting. You could help me. Okay?"

"Go away!"

He threw his pillow to the ground. He kicked it, sending it flying against his closet. He punched the air. He threw himself back onto his bed. He was wheezing. His asthma. It was his mother's fault. She gave it to him.

He took his spray out of his pocket, pushed all the air out of his lungs, stuck the nozzle into his mouth, and depressed the cannister. The cool mist shot down his throat into his lungs. He was supposed to hold his breath, with the mist inside his lungs, for fifteen seconds. That's how long it usually took for the medicine to work. He remembered being taught how to take the spray, being taught by his mother how to hold his breath. This time, he would hold his breath for two minutes. He could do that. She couldn't make him breathe. Nobody could.

After thirty seconds he pinched his nose closed with his fingers. He sucked his top lip into his mouth. He clenched his teeth.

His heart began to punch against the inside of his chest. He felt a dull throbbing ache behind his ears.

He wasn't going to breathe. Let Mr. Macombo come in and tell him to. Let his father come back from Chicago and tell him. He wasn't going to breathe until he was ready. He wasn't going into any special class. He wasn't going to be special anymore. It was his life. He could do what he wanted with it.

Little black specks floated across the room. His arms were trembling. He felt dizzy.

The air exploded out of his mouth. He began to cough and sneeze fitfully. His throat burned. Slowly the pounding inside his chest began to subside. The black spots faded away. His vision became clear. Everything in his room suddenly seemed sharp and definite, separate from everything else. His chair, his desk, each pencil and pen in the mug on his desk. His room was filled with things. There were his and Isaac's blue Rangers jerseys hanging on their closet door; there were their hockey sticks standing upside down in the corner, their blades curved, thinned and shedding fiberglass. There were his black skates with their undone laces; there was his model of Henry Hudson's *Half Moon*, painted chocolate brown with white sails. There was his model of the Bride of Frankenstein, her crazy grey hair sizzling straight up, her eyes bloody red. There were all these things. Separate, not belonging.

He was leaving. He wasn't going back to the way things used to be. He would hate himself. He took a notebook from his desk and began to write his mother a letter.

He began with the Night Sky of Kansas. He wrote about waking up that morning exhausted but wanting to get to school. He wrote how his mother and Isaac had stopped him. How they had ruined his chance to start the year off just like a regular kid in a regular class. He wrote down everything they said. He wrote down what he had said as well. He skipped lines between the speakers, just as the authors did in the plays his parents read.

He found himself laughing at his own words. He was clever. He wrote about his conversation with the clerk at the bookstore where he purchased the Sky. He wrote about meeting Theodore. He wrote down every word the two of them had said. He wrote about his first day of school, of the stupid things Ms. Brace had said, what each of the kids had said in their essays.

He wanted his mother to understand, to see what she and his father and Isaac had put him through, how bad it had been. He wanted her to see that she didn't know who he really was.

His mother brought in a new dinner. He ignored it, continuing to write about why he was running away. Writing, he discovered, made him feel powerful. He had control over what happened. He started to change things a little, making the scenes in his life more dramatic, his enemies a little more evil, his own words and actions more admirable. When he changed things, they seemed more like the truth.

Isaac came home. He mentioned to Jacob something about his play, about how much he had to memorize. Jacob ignored him and reread to himself what he had written. He was amused and proud to discover he had made himself into some sort of hero. He had battled so many obstacles! He was like a little Jewish Hercules, only funnier.

Isaac said something to him about the Mets, then left

the room when Jacob didn't respond. When he returned, he climbed up to his top bunk.

Jacob ignored him. He began to write about walking with his father in the museum. He wrote how he had asked his father to stay, and how his father had said no.

At some point Isaac turned off his light. Writing by his own tiny light, Jacob imagined the morning, imagined what could have happened.

She is standing on top of a hill beneath a tree, he wrote. *It is quiet. She is wearing black pants and a little black jacket. She smiles when I approach. She turns on the tape player. . . .*

He couldn't write anymore. He put down his pen and got out of bed to pack. He quietly removed his hockey-equipment bag from the bottom of his closet. He silently emptied it, then brought it over to his dresser and pulled open his medicine drawer. He quickly began to pack his sprays and pills and sticky cough-syrup bottles. He found copies of his prescriptions, which he neatly folded and tucked into the corner of his bag.

Next he went over to his bookshelf and removed all of his favorite mysteries and science-fiction novels and placed them neatly into the bag. He found his copy of *Legends of Crime* on Isaac's desk. He placed it in the bag's outer pocket, where he usually kept his hockey gloves.

He couldn't figure out what to pack next, so he opened up his underwear drawer and picked out four clean pairs of undershorts and ten pairs of his favorite tube socks.

He began to cry. He got up and dressed. He put on his black pants and the white shirt he had worn to meet Cynthia. He couldn't find his black high-tops, so he put on his old white high-tops instead. He sat down at his desk and looked out of his window at the dark, lifeless buildings across the street. He turned on his desk light and reread what he had written in his notebook. It was almost a play. He reread the parts with Cynthia.

As the sun began to rise, he grabbed his notebook and left. He was going to find her.

14

Sitting on a grassy hill overlooking the 89th Street ball-field, Jacob was amused by two mad squirrels who chased each other from base to base. He wished he had brought his pen. He was alone, with nothing else to do, and Central Park seemed like a poem. When he was younger, he listened to his father recite poems to him at bedtime. Often the images from the poems had become his dreams.

With the islands of mist silently floating about the park, and with the red, brown, and golden leaves of the trees fluttering in the warm breeze, Jacob felt very dreamy. If he had his pen, he could write a poem and give it to Cynthia when she came. He could give it to her along with his book if she came. *When* she came.

All he had with him was his story. He didn't know why. The story seemed enough, although he would certainly need his medicines wherever he went. He would also miss his books. He had written the story for his mother. But when it was finished, Jacob realized he needed to give it to Cynthia, to show her something about himself before he left.

The traffic above and behind him on Central Park West

sounded like waves drifting in and out of the city. Suddenly, as if seized by an urge to fly, one of the squirrels leapt straight up into the air. The other scrambled away and up a tree. The squirrel leapt again and again.

"Hey, where were you yesterday? You were supposed to be here."

Jacob spun around.

"You know, I waited for you for an hour. I was late to school, and when I got there, everybody made fun of me because I was dressed so nicely. What happened to you?"

Jacob stood up and offered Cynthia his hand. She was carrying a large portable cassette player. She gently put it down and held out her hand. Jacob took it and held it for a few seconds. It was cool and soft. He wanted to laugh, to shout, to jump up and down. He shook her hand.

"Hiya, Cynthia," he said. "I wrote you something."

"You wore nice clothes," Cynthia said, looking him over. "You're all in black and white. You look really old-fashioned. Like Fred Astaire. Except for your sneakers."

"They used to be my best sneakers," Jacob apologized.

"No, they're nice," Cynthia admitted. "It's just that Fred Astaire never wore high-tops. But that's okay. When you become good, we'll buy you tap shoes. What's that?" she asked, pointing to his notebook.

"It's my story. I wrote it. It's for you. I didn't write it for you, at first, but now it's for you. You're in it. I made you sound clever and pretty. I think I'm going to be running away. I wanted you to keep it. You look pretty in real life, too."

Cynthia took the notebook from Jacob, opened it to the first page, and read softly to herself. Watching her expression turn serious, Jacob stepped forward and turned to the page where he first mentioned her. He stepped back. With a feeling of giddy pleasure he watched her smile as she read his description of her. She closed the book and tucked it under her arm.

"So where do you want to dance?" she asked.

Jacob shrugged his shoulders.

"Well, it's too hilly up here," she said, surveying the park. "Why don't we go down there, by those trees."

"It's kind of foggy down there, isn't it? It would be like walking into a cloud."

"What's the matter. You afraid we'll disappear?"

"No. I'd like that."

"Good. Then let's go. We don't have much time. We'll have to start with the easy steps." She picked up the cassette player. "Thanks for the book, Jacob," she said. "It makes me feel . . ." Instead of finishing, she reached out for his hand and led him down the hill.

The fog was wet and grey, and as they entered into it, the rest of the park disappeared into a grey blur. Except for the wet leaves and the grass beneath his feet, Jacob felt as if they could have been in a cloud, drifting across the sky.

There was no need to run away. This cloud could be his home.

"Now, don't worry if you feel clumsy," Cynthia said, putting down the cassette player. "You're really not going to look good next to me for a while. Remember, I've been practicing this for almost a year. And I've seen all the movies. I'm almost an expert."

He was never going to let go of her hand.

"Well," she corrected herself. "I'm really more like a 'watching expert.' I'm not a dancing expert, yet. It'll take us years before we really get that good."

With her free hand she snapped in the cassette and pressed play. A scratchy hissing came out of the speakers, followed by a bright piano melody.

Cynthia stepped up to him, took his right hand, and placed it on the small of her back. He was close enough to kiss her. The thought made him dizzy.

"Take a step back," she suggested. "We're too close. You'll step on my toes."

He couldn't speak. He couldn't tell her that he would never step on her toes.

"First we'll start with the simple waltz stuff," she said. "Just follow me."

They began to dance.

15

an I have my notebook back?" Jacob asked as they returned to the top of the hill.

"No," Cynthia said.

"I'll give it back to you," he assured her. "I just need to add another scene. I want to change what I wrote about today."

"No," Cynthia said. "I'm going to give it back to you? You're going to run away. I'll never see you again. Nobody's ever given me something like this before. Nobody's ever written about me. And besides, you write better than you talk. I'm not giving it back to you. I'll never see you again."

"Aren't we going to rehearse again tomorrow?"

"How? You're running away."

"No, I'm not. I'm not going anywhere," Jacob said. "I want to do this every day. I want to come back here and rehearse with you."

"I'm not giving it back," Cynthia smiled.

"I just want to rewrite today," Jacob explained. "I want to write about the squirrels I saw playing down on the field before you came. I want to write about dancing and disappearing in the fog. I want to write more of you."

"Then start something new. Write something that shows what we were like when we were children—before we became famous."

Jacob laughed, then began to cough. For a second he lost his breath.

"You all right?" Cynthia asked, looking worried.

"I'm just a little allergic to the park," Jacob said, bending over, pressing his fists down on his thighs. He took a deep breath. He was wheezing.

"We'd better get out of the park. You're not sounding too good," Cynthia said, picking up her radio. "It's almost 7:30, and I have to go home and change before school. You'd better change too, or everybody will make fun of you."

"Wait," Jacob said, taking in a deep breath. He took his spray. He held his breath for a few seconds, then exhaled. His lungs were clear. "Can I meet you? I'll walk you to school."

"You can't have your book back."

"I'll meet you on the corner of 89th and Broadway. At the newsstand. I want to introduce you to somebody."

"Just be there by eight."

"I'll be there," Jacob said.

"You know," Cynthia said, backing away towards the exit. "They put me in Ms. Brace's class."

"That was the class I was supposed to be in," Jacob called to her.

"Well, gotta dance!" she sang.

He watched her run uptown. When he could no longer see her, he pictured her walking into that class without him.

He would walk her to school. But what would he do once he got there?

He began to cough. He was wheezing again. He took his spray. He waited a few seconds, then exhaled.

"Gotta dance!" he shouted to the park. "Gotta dance!"

He ran back to his apartment.

16

Neither his mother nor his brother was awake when he got back to his apartment. Quickly and quietly he shoved his equipment sack under his bed. He changed his clothes. He was nervous and eager. He was going to walk Cynthia to school. Then he was going to walk her up to Ms. Brace's class. Then he was going to sit down next to her.

Cynthia wasn't going into that class without him. She was his partner. It didn't matter what class his parents put him in. He was going back to Ms. Brace's class just as if it were his first day of school. He would forget what those kids had thought, what they had written about him. He could prove he was just like them, just as tough. He would forget what Ms. Brace had done. Or ignore her. He wasn't running away from anything anymore. He began to lace up his new black high-tops.

Isaac's alarm went off. So did his mother's. Jacob grabbed his books and knocked on his mother's door.

"Where are you going?" his mother asked.

"School," Jacob said.

"I think that's a very good idea." She smiled.

"Me too."

"And, Jacob, I know you're going to like this class. You're going to be surprised."

"I think you will be too."

"Did you eat breakfast?"

"Yes. It was great," he lied.

He ran down the five flights of steps and reached the street door of his building before he remembered his spray. He had left it in the front pocket of his "dancing pants." He thought about running upstairs for it, but he was afraid he would miss Cynthia. He shut the door behind him and began to jog up the block. He wasn't going to be late. He was going to introduce her to Theodore. Then he was going to walk to school with her.

From a distance he could see somebody, a kid, talking to Theodore. He rubbed his eyes. They were a little blurry and itchy. He was allergic to that park.

Approaching the stand, he saw it was Cynthia. She was leaning against it, wearing a flowery dress and a beret. She had a drink in her hand. She saw him and waved.

It was becoming a little more difficult to breathe. His skin was beginning to feel hot and itchy. He rubbed his eyes. They wouldn't stop tearing. He took a deep breath.

"Hiya, Cynthia. Hiya, Theodore," he said.

"How you doing there, Dillinger?" Theodore asked. "Your friend just introduced herself to me."

"Great," Jacob laughed, then began to cough.

"Hey, are you all right?" Cynthia asked, sounding alarmed. "Maybe you should take that spray."

"No," Jacob said, shaking his head. "I'll be fine. There's nothing wrong with me."

"You want some of my juice? I just bought it with my pistachios. It's my breakfast."

"That's not a very healthy breakfast, young lady," Theodore said sternly.

"My father forgot to go shopping last night," Cynthia said. "He sort of fell asleep."

Jacob took the can of juice from Cynthia. The straw was scarlet from the nuts. He took a sip. It was apple juice. It reminded him of home. As it cooled his throat, he tasted something unusual—the pistachios. He remembered what happened the last time he had experienced that taste, the last time he had swallowed something that had come in contact with the oils from nuts. He had almost died.

17

It wasn't the first time he had woken up within the clear plastic sheeting of an oxygen tent. The hum of the clean air being pumped into the tent, the stinging sensation in his right forearm where a tube entered his skin carrying the sugar water to his veins, were familiar and comforting. They reassured him that he was alive. He sat up. His arms trembled from the effort. He took in a deep breath through his nose. The cool air inside the tent seemed electrically charged. It made his chest tingle.

"You know you can't eat pistachio nuts, Jacob. You know you can't. You know they set off your asthma."

"Dad?"

His father was sitting in a chair beside the bed. His eyes were bloodshot. His grey hair was uncombed, and he needed a shave. His sweatshirt was inside out. His face was long and drawn, and he looked tiny in his clothes.

"Since when can you eat pistachios? You can't forget these things, Jacob. This is your life." His father rubbed his eyes with a balled-up tissue, then wiped his nose.

"I didn't eat the pistachios, Dad. . . ." Jacob began to cry.

His father stuffed the tissue into his pocket, rose from

his chair, parted the sheeting of the tent, and climbed inside. He sat down at the edge of the bed, put his arm around Jacob, and kissed him on the top of his head.

"So . . . so this is your idea of camping?" his father asked, touching the walls of the tent. "Any problems with bears?"

"Barely," Jacob laughed.

"Hmm," his father inhaled deeply. "I must say, the air is fresh."

"You look terrible," Jacob said. His throat burned when he spoke.

His father smiled, removed the messy tissue ball from his pocket, spilling drinking-straw papers, pretzel crumbs, cookie pieces, and other tissue strands along with it. He looked old, older than he had looked in the museum.

"Where's Mom?" Jacob asked.

"She just took your brother for some food. We were all sitting here last night, watching you sleep. It was fun. It was just like watching one of your mother's plays."

Jacob laughed again. But his chest ached. He felt as if he had been beaten.

"What are you doing here?" he asked.

"Move over, son," his father said, putting his feet up on the bed. His shoes were off. He was wearing a blue sock on his left foot, a dark green one on his right.

"Your socks don't match," Jacob said, sliding over.

"You know the advantage of a clear tent?" his father asked, dropping his head onto one of Jacob's pillows. He crossed his hands on his chest. "You can see the stars come out at night."

"Did Isaac tell you about the Night Sky over Kansas?"

"Yes." His father smiled. "He said it was one of the

nicest things you had ever done for him. I figured it was one of your pranks, but I didn't say anything. I didn't want to ruin his image of you."

"I must have really scared him this time."

"You did."

Jacob laid down next to his father. Everything ached, his back, his chest, his fingers.

"Jacob, your mother and I have decided that you're not going into any Special 10 class. If you need any special help, we'll both work with you. I'm not going back to Chicago."

Jacob pushed himself up on his elbows.

"And I'm not going back to acting, either," his father said.

"What are you going to do?" Jacob asked.

"Lie down with my son, out here in the wilderness. Breathe deeply. Listen for bear. Wait for the stars to come out."

18

The doctor, a young balding man with red glasses, entered, reading a chart. When he looked up, he nearly dropped it. Jacob's father was still asleep under the tent. Beside the bed Jacob sat in the visitor's chair, reading the sports section of the *Chicago Tribune*. The intravenous tube was still connected to his arm.

"Wait a second. Who's the patient here?" the doctor asked, amused.

"That's my father," Jacob said proudly. "He just flew in from Chicago."

"Looks like he made an emergency landing," the doctor laughed.

Jacob looked over at his father and laughed too.

The doctor, who was also wearing red sneakers, said Jacob would have to wake his father soon. Then he pulled up another chair and asked Jacob some questions about how he was feeling and scribbled Jacob's responses onto his chart. He gave Jacob a cylinder to blow into that was connected by a tube to a radio-size machine. The machine was designed to measure his lung capacity. Jacob blew. The reading was good. His lungs were nearly back to normal. With his cold stethoscope the doctor listened to Jacob's heart and lungs. More good news.

The nurse entered. Seeing Jacob's father out cold in the tent, she became flustered.

"He just flew in from Chicago," the doctor informed her.

"Crash landing," Jacob added.

"I didn't see him come in," she apologized to the doctor.

"You didn't check the windows," the doctor joked. He patted Jacob on the back. "Everything's looking good," he said. He showed the nurse the chart and, after a few minutes, waved good-bye. He left the nurse to take blood from Jacob's right thumb.

After the nurse left, Jacob returned to his visitor's chair and waited for his mother and Isaac to return. When they arrived a few minutes later, their grave looks broke into smiles. His mother hugged him, careful not to disconnect the intravenous tube. Isaac went to hug him, but shook his hand instead.

"Here." He handed Jacob a book.

"*More Legends of Crime*," Jacob read aloud. He opened the book to its table of contents.

"I checked," Isaac said. "You're not in it."

"Thanks, Isaac."

"Isaac, please get us some chairs," his mother asked. Isaac left the room. "Jacob, you'll probably be able to come home tomorrow." His mother squeezed his hand.

"When can I go back to school?"

"Your father told you our decision?"

"Yes."

"You were right, Jacob," she admitted. "You'll be happier in a regular classroom."

116

"So when can I go back?"

His mother looked at him curiously. "I guess in a few days. I don't want you to exert yourself too soon."

Isaac returned, carrying a chair in each hand. His face was pale, his eyes red. He had been crying.

"Stop it!" Jacob ordered. "I'm going to be fine. We'll be able to watch television later. There's a good Japanese monster film on at seven. It's dubbed."

Isaac laughed. "Now that Dad's back, maybe he can teach you how to box," Isaac suggested, removing his jacket. He looked around for a place to hang it.

"Why? You don't think I can defend myself?" Jacob asked.

"Not against me," Isaac laughed, approaching the bed. He parted the sheets of the oxygen tent and covered their father with his jacket.

"Dillinger?"

It was Theodore. He was standing in the doorway, wearing a shiny blue sports jacket and a tie. Cynthia was holding his hand. She was wearing a pair of jeans and a new sweatshirt. She was carrying a silver gift-wrapped package with a bow on it.

"Hey, Dillinger." Theodore smiled broadly. "If you ask me, you're looking much better," he laughed.

"Thanks." Jacob laughed along with him. "But I don't think anybody's going to ask you."

"Hi," Cynthia said. "This is Theodore. I'm Jacob's partner," she told Jacob's mother and Isaac. "So when are you coming back to school?" she asked Jacob.

"Monday, before anybody gets a chance to write me a get-well card. And I want to get right back to rehearsing." He noticed she was wearing her clock earrings. Suddenly he remembered he was wearing a white hospital robe. He looked down at his bare feet, embarrassed.

"Don't worry," she reassured him. "Even Fred had to take off his taps once in a while. Anyway, I brought you something. Theodore helped me out. Here." She offered him the package.

"Thanks," Jacob said, removing the wrapping. It was a thick black-leather-covered book. It had no title. Its pages were blank.

"And this," she added, handing him a silver pen. "Since I'm never giving you back your notebook, I thought I could replace it. I thought you might want to start writing something new."

"I do." Jacob flipped through the book's blank pages. "I was thinking that I wanted to start writing about what we were like before we were famous."

"Hey, I can help you with that," Cynthia offered.

"You can," Jacob agreed.

Stealthy as thieves, Jacob and Cynthia waited by the Milky Way Room for the guard to turn left and head down the hallway. They had spent the last few hours in the planetarium, timing him. He wouldn't be back for another twenty minutes. Quietly, secretly, Cynthia placed her small tape player beneath the rings of Saturn. Looking up at Jacob, she bit her lip to avoid laughing, then pressed play. A thick, crackly voice began to sing along with what sounded like a toy orchestra. Jacob looked up at the arched ceiling and its painted constellations. He took Cynthia's hand.

"One, two, three, four," Cynthia counted off, and they began to dance.

He was going to school tomorrow. With Cynthia.

"I wonder what would have happened if you'd been allergic to the Milky Way?" Cynthia asked. She extended her arm up into the air and spun gracefully past a meteor shower to Jupiter.

"We would have traveled to another galaxy," Jacob explained. He waited for her to twirl back to him. He counted to himself—as she had instructed—to eight. When he finished, she was back in his arms, and they were gliding past the Earth.

"I couldn't have gone there without you," she said. "I don't have a bus pass." They stepped towards the moon. "Keep counting," she reminded him as they waltzed past the moon's dark side. "You nervous about tomorrow?"

"No. You're going to be there," he told her. "Ouch!"

He had bumped into the case containing the moon rock.

"We're lucky there's no life on Mars," Cynthia sighed, looking up at the red planet, "or they'd be laughing at us."

The song ended. Cynthia knelt down by the tape recorder and pressed rewind. Jacob moaned and rubbed his back.

"It doesn't matter what Ms. Brace told them about me. I'm just a regular kid."

"And my partner," Cynthia added.

"They'll find out about me soon enough. Tomorrow's my first day of school. I'm going to start everything all over again."

"Me too," Cynthia said as she pressed play.

Jacob stepped forward and took her hand. They looked up at the night sky glittering above them. The air was cool and clear. It was easy to breathe.

"One . . . two . . . three . . . four," Cynthia counted.

And the song began again.